PICKETT'S CHARGE

"I've been lookin' for you," Pickett said, the sound of his voice like a grate on Billy's nerves. "Somebody told me you'd hightailed it out of town."

From the corner of his eye Billy saw Asa creep toward the front of the chuck wagon, staying behind it. "That somebody was wrong," he said, rocking back on his boot heels just a little to keep his knees from trembling. "I'm right here. No need to look any longer . . ."

"Funny," Pickett remarked, without grinning. "I had you pegged for a yellow bastard. Figured it was whiskey doin' all that big talkin' last night."

"I'd had a few. But it was me doin' the talking. I ain't yellow, an' I sure as hell ain't no bastard, either. If you've got business with me, let's get it settled."

The gunman nodded and swung down from his horse, keeping a close eye on Billy's gun hand . . . "We've got unfinished business, you an' me. You called me a backshooter in front of everybody at Belle's. That don't leave me no choice but to kill you from the front side, to prove you was wrong."

Again, the sudden dryness occurred in his mouth. "You make it sound like killin' me is gonna be easy . . ."

RIDING FOR THE BRAND

J. M. Thompson

RIDING FOR THE BRAND

A Berkley Book / published by arrangement with the author

PRINTING HISTORY
Berkley edition / March 1999

The Penguin Putnam Inc. World Wide Web site address is
http://www.penguinputnam.com

ISBN: 0-425-16778-X

BERKLEY®
Berkley Books are published by The Berkley Publishing Group,
a member of Penguin Putnam Inc.,
375 Hudson Street, New York, New York 10014.
BERKLEY and the "B" logo
are trademarks belonging to Berkley Publishing Corporation.

PRINTED IN THE UNITED STATES OF AMERICA

10 9 8 7 6 5 4 3 2 1

To Terri

RIDING FOR THE BRAND

ONE

On the last page of the family Bible, where the offspring of Nathaniel and Martha Blue were listed, his full name was given as William Jackson Blue. He had been called Billy since he first saw light of day, with the exception of those times when his mother was after him with a razor strap or a mesquite switch, or when Nathaniel was on a similar prod over something Billy had done wrong, or failed to do, such as chores. When Billy heard his full name being called, it always produced the same response, out of habit, after having his backside tanned so often when it was used. He hid. Or ran. Sometimes both. It wasn't that he was all that inclined toward mischievousness, really. Nathaniel and Martha held firm to the belief that children needed regular strappings. Nathaniel cited scripture as justification for it, the claim that sparing the rod would spoil a child. Thus Billy was certain he hadn't been spoiled, since whippings came his way regularly, until he was old enough to run away from home to join the army. When the call went out for loyal Texans to join up with Hood's Brigades, Billy signed the paper willingly, convinced that war could hardly be much worse than Nathaniel Blue's razor strap or farm chores. All too soon Billy discovered he'd been wrong about that particular notion. War was a hell from which he would never fully recover, like thousands of other Confederate veterans who somehow survived it. Ghosts from that experience still haunted him, robbing him of sleep, and there were times when only the bottom of a whiskey bottle provided a remedy for long strings of sleepless nights.

Such was the case when fate brought him to Fort Worth in the spring of '72, to a district known as Hell's Half Acre, where the saloons and whorehouses so greatly outnumbered the churches that city fathers annually considered a ban on further development of sin parlors until more houses of worship could be built. But grim economic reality was on the side of sin in a city strategically placed at the jumping-off spot for the Chisholm Trail across Indian Territory. Cattle shepherds faced with months of deprivation needed fortification for long cattle drives, and Fort Worth merchants sought to provide every form of sinful diversion known to man, as well as other necessities of a cowboy's life. Billy Blue was drawn to Hell's Half Acre by the same natural urges other cowboys harkened to, thus it was not by accident that he found himself there just as the big herds were being formed on the prairies north and west of town, to begin the arduous spring drives to Kansas railheads.

These same fates also summoned a man of particularly intemperate disposition to the saloon district that spring. Hell's Half Acre was known to attract men of his ilk, for they preyed on men of lesser skill with cards, dice, and guns. Crooked gamblers and shootists frequented the gaming parlors and bawdy houses during cow season, for this was where drunken cowboys provided the easiest pickings. If a rowdy cowboy under the influence of too much red-eye whiskey could not be taken for his money by gentler means, it was not uncommon for a gun or a knife to accomplish the task. A certain amount of bloodshed was tolerated by local officials in the district, just so long as it did not spread to quieter parts of the city. With this type of official forbearance, Fort Worth sometimes became a gathering ground for desperate men wanted by the law in other places. As was the case in '72, when a killer by the name of Leon Pickett came to town. Pickett was said to have outgunned nine men in fair fights with pistols since the war ended, and rumor had it that he had killed perhaps a dozen more by less virtuous means. His reputation with a gun was more than sufficient to keep most men fearful and cautious when in his company. It was the misfortune of William Jackson Blue that he knew nothing about Leon Pickett's deadly reputation when they met at the Pink Garter on a cool night early in March. Their meeting was by happenstance, over a woman . . .

"You're a right pretty lady," Billy said.

The buxom maiden might have blushed. He'd have been able to tell if the light had been better, but he was sure that he saw color in her cheeks when she replied demurely, "I am told that, sometimes, but I only keep company with the most handsome men, like yourself, cowboy."

"My name's Billy. Billy Blue."

She smiled. "Right unusual, to have a color for a name. I reckon the same can be said for Green. There's lots of Greens, but not nearly so many Blues." She laughed.

"I asked my pa about that once. He said most men of our clan have met with heavy doses of misfortune. Lots of us Blues got killed in the war against England. Leastways that's what he told me the time I asked, ma'am."

"You can call me Ann. And if you like, you can buy me a drink. I prefer wine, red wine. Women of refinement are wine drinkers, in case you didn't know."

"I could tell right off you were a lady of refinement," he told her, knowing otherwise, having found her in a whorehouse. But he would grant her that, thinking she was refined. In the end it would make no difference, unless refined whores cost more money. He examined her face again, her blond hair hanging down her neck, where sweat from a hot, crowded room wilted her curls. He supposed he could call her pretty, since he was in a generous mood. Her low-cut red satin gown revealed ample bosom that jiggled when she moved, and her breasts were dewy with tiny drops of perspiration. The sight stirred him. "I'll order you a glass of red wine, an' a whiskey for myself. I never did lay no claim to bein' all that refined." He signaled a bartender and waited for the chance to place his order, casting a careless glance around the place, passing time until drinks arrived. He'd been needing more whiskey of late just to get to sleep.

"It's awfully hot in here," she said, fanning herself with a paper fan decorated by a border of lace. "It's cooler upstairs in a corner room like mine . . ."

It occurred to him that Ann wasn't one for wasting any time. "It sure is hot. That room sounds nice. Cooler."

She feigned brief annoyance then. "It's a rule of the house that when a lady takes a gentleman upstairs, the gentleman has to pay for the room, if you know what I mean."

"I know what you mean. A rule of the house. I've heard it called that before . . ."

Ann smiled again. "It's only ten dollars, and the price does include having me . . . having your way with me, if you care to indulge yourself in such a manner."

"I'd sure as hell like that part, only the price sounds a bit too high, maybe. I ain't used to payin' more'n six or seven for a room. Now, I ain't sayin' you aren't worth that much, but it sounds kinda high for the room. Don't get me wrong. It's the room that's on the high side of things."

Her smile faded quickly. "Are you broke, cowboy? Because if you are, then you can't afford me."

He shrugged. It was the truth that he was almost busted, down to twenty dollars in his poke, but then he would never admit to it. "I'm flush as a baby pig on a frosty mornin', Miss Ann. It's the price for the room that don't sound right to me. If I had all the money in the world, the room would still be too high priced for my tastes. Hell, it's only a room."

There was a hint of impatience in her voice when she said, "It includes being intimate with me. I want you to know I am a very discriminating woman. I won't allow intimacy if a man does not bathe regularly, or if he cavorts with low-bred women who may carry social diseases."

"I'd never consider bedding down with women like that. I reckon you could say I'm real discriminating myself when it comes to womenfolk. They have to be pretty, like you, an' I'd need to be sure they wasn't carryin' the pox or anything of that nature."

Ann regarded him a moment, as though she might be considering a slight reduction in her price. "You are a very handsome man," she said later, lowering her voice. "Under special circumstances I occasionally make exceptions. Because you are clearly a gentleman, I suppose I might be talked into sharing my room with you for eight dollars, but I'd have to have your word that you wouldn't tell a soul about it."

"I'd swear it on my own sister's grave," he said, feeling safe from God's wrath since he had no sister, only brothers.

Ann's brow furrowed. "How did your sister die?" she asked with what sounded like genuine concern.

He had time to think of an answer while a bartender arrived to take his request for a glass of red wine and a shot of good whiskey. Counting out money for the drinks, he said, "She died of grief, I was told. I wasn't there when she passed on, but I was told she suffered a terrible grief when our pa got kicked in the head by a mule. Pa never was the same after that. Pissed in his pants now and then and couldn't remember his own name, or where he was most of the time." It was true that Nathaniel had been kicked in the head by his own brown mule, but the blow was slight and Billy couldn't tell if it changed his pa's disposition all that greatly, being he was mean-spirited in the first place. Meaner than the brown mule, anyways.

"I'm so sorry," Ann remarked. "I'll take your word that it will be our secret about the price of my room tonight, since you gave an oath on your deceased sister's grave."

"I'd never take a thing like a dead sister lightly."

"I understand. It was a very gentlemanly thing to say and I believe your word is good."

Their drinks arrived, a glass of pinkish wine in a crystal goblet and an amber shot glass full of watered whiskey.

"We can take our drinks upstairs," Ann offered, indicating a stairway across the parlor. She lowered her voice again when she added, "but you must pay for the room before we go. It's a rule of the house . . ."

He nodded that he understood, taking eight silver dollars from his pocket reluctantly, for the money would seem precious if he couldn't find work soon. With less than ten dollars to his name after making the investment in a whore and drinks, he would soon face starvation unless his luck changed.

But when he glanced down at the cleft between Ann's generous breasts, his decision was easily made. He paid her and picked up his whiskey at the very same moment that a hush spread across the front parlor of the Pink Garter. Everyone in the place seemed to be watching the front door as a man in a black suit coat and tall stovepipe boots paused in the door frame. A black flat-brim hat with a layer of trail dust on it covered most of his face with shadows cast by lamp fixtures above the door. Only a clean-shaven chin and a waxed handlebar mustache showed below his drooping hat brim in the half dark where he stood. It was then that Billy's eyes fell to the gunbelt around the newcomer's waist, a holster tied low on his leg in the fashion of a man who fancied himself a gunfighter.

Ann's attention was on the stranger, too, and just then Billy heard her gasp quietly, lifting a palm to cover her mouth and her surprise.

"Who's that?" Billy asked, puzzled by the sudden silence in a room that was full of noise moments earlier.

Ann turned to him, and some of the color was missing from her face. "That's Leon Pickett. Here's your money back. Sorry, but Leon will be asking for me." She handed him the silver and made to leave the bar, until Billy grabbed her arm.

"Hold on a minute," he said. "I already paid for an evening with you, Miss Ann. Whoever Leon Pickett is, he can wait."

The woman's eyes rounded a little. "You don't understand, do you? Haven't you heard about Leon? Who he is?"

Billy wagged his head. "Never heard the name before, but it wouldn't make no difference. You already took that money from me an' I don't want it back."

Ann stared at him, like she couldn't quite believe what he said. "You've never heard of Leon Pickett?"

"Never." He glanced to the doorway again. "Who the hell is he anyway?"

"Just about the meanest man this cow town has ever seen. I can't figure why you never heard of him before." Her voice was a whisper now. "He's a killer, Billy. Please take your money and go away or there'll be trouble."

Perhaps it was the result of too much whiskey when he said, "I never was one to shy away from trouble, pretty lady. I paid you for the room and your company tonight. This Pickett feller can wait his turn."

"You don't understand," Ann spat angrily, but without saying it too loud. "He came here to see me . . ."

"I don't give a damn if he rode a thousand miles. I paid my money an' you took it first. He can wait."

The woman's stare turned cold. "Leon don't wait for nobody. He'd just as soon kill you as sneeze."

It was the challenge he didn't like and he said so. "I've been told I'm mighty hard to kill. Plenty of Yankees tried it an' couldn't get it done."

"Leon isn't just some Yankee soldier. He hires out his gun to whoever pays the most. He's a paid killer, Billy. Take your money and go away before trouble starts. Come back tomorrow . . ."

Billy made a half turn away from the bar. Whiskey made his tongue looser than it should have been. "That just wouldn't be my style," he said, watching Pickett, the angle of his gun in a cutaway holster. "Tell him he can come back tomorrow."

It was then that Pickett noticed him standing beside Ann at the back of the Pink Garter. Pickett raised his head slightly so their eyes met. Billy felt something cold forming in the pit of his stomach, like he'd swallowed a ball of ice. But despite the chill in his belly when he looked at the gunman, he reached for the front of Ann's red gown and dropped his money down between her breasts, into her corset.

The woman drew in a quick breath. A corner of Leon Pickett's mouth lifted, a one-sided grin lasting only a second or two as he swept the tail of his frock coat away from the butt of his Colt revolver, just before he took the first step toward Billy.

TWO

He watched Pickett walk across the room, wondering if this would be his appointment with death, one he had narrowly escaped so many times during four long years with Hood. Not until he came face-to-face with death during the war was he truly able to grasp its finality. He'd begun soldiering as a boy of sixteen, fresh off a dry-land farm with no firsthand knowledge of guns or dying beyond an old hunting shotgun his father owned, and having attended his grandpa's funeral at the age of twelve. Death was a pine casket and a waxy body without breath in its lungs, wrapped in a purple blanket provided by the undertaker. His grandpa had been old, eighty-six, and Nathaniel Blue told everyone it had been time for him to die. Thus death was something with an appointed time, in Billy's youthful view, until he marched his way to the battle of Bull Run with Hood's Confederate Army.

His first infantry charge began as an exhilarating experience after marching hundreds of miles to reach the battlefront. Dressed in a fine gray uniform, armed with his own musket and shot and a fixed bayonet, he felt fully grown. He remembered thinking then how he could finally call himself a man now. His two newest and closest friends, Asa Carter and Jessie Small, were running beside him having a wonderful time dressed up like soldiers, and right at that moment, at Manassas Junction, Virginia, on Sunday morning the 21st of July in 1861, Billy Blue wouldn't have traded soldiering for any other profession in the world. Screaming hatred for men whom he knew nothing about, other than they were called Yankees, he made ready to kill his first man during the heat of battle. He was certain he could do it. The morning air had a crisp, fresh smell despite the scent of gunpowder, and the shouts mingling with loud musket blasts were so exciting. A flag bearer ran off to the left carrying the banner of the Texas Brigades. A deep pride for that flag had been instilled in every soldier by General Hood himself the day before, when he spoke to his men about the forthcoming engagement. Billy had hardly slept at all that night, nor had Asa or Jessie, awaiting their first real experience as fighting men.

And at the appointed hour, as the order to charge was given up and down the lines of waiting infantrymen, Billy's heartbeat quickened and his mouth felt dry, cottony. His hands began to sweat holding the walnut stock of his rifle. A tiny tremor in his fingers made it more difficult to hold his musket steady as men in gray started across the meadow toward Yankee positions at the tops of the hills. Soon everyone was running, and some were screaming, and thus he added his own thin voice to the shrill chorus of yells coming from Confederate lines. He could hear Asa above all the others, shrieking like a hunted peafowl as he dashed up the first hillside. Jessie ran faster than anyone else in the company, racing to the front of the line as though he meant to be the first soldier from Waco to kill a Yankee today. Billy saw Jessie jump over a rotted tree trunk with his rifle against his shoulder. Then Jessie Small met his appointment with destiny, a musket ball ending his glorious charge with a suddenness Jessie never had the chance to fully comprehend.

The back of Jessie's gray tunic erupted when the shot passed through him. Billy watched his friend's strides falter without understanding why Jessie's legs refused to work. A hole the size of Billy's fist spewed dark blood over the grass, marking a trail Jessie made toward the hilltop. Staggering, clutching his musket to his breast, Jessie managed a few wobbly steps more and sank to his knees. Blood pumped from the hole in his back, squirting red fluid in regular bursts down his buttocks and legs, covering his new marching boots. Kneeling thus, he appeared to be praying on the hillside while soldiers swarmed past him. He finally relaxed his grip on the rifle and let it fall to the ground in front of him just when Billy reached his side.

"Jessie! You're shot!" Billy had cried that day, feeling a rush of hot tears flood his cheeks.

Jessie's deep blue eyes turned on Billy, and in them Billy saw his friend's terrible pain, an agony so deep that no words were needed. Dark pools formed slowly at the centers of his eyes as Jessie knelt, trembling, bleeding, edging closer to death yet still unwilling to fall. His lips started to move, but no sound came from them. Pink froth rolled down the tip of his tongue and fell on the front of his tunic where the musket ball had entered his chest, puckering his new uniform into a bloody socket tucked inside the wound.

"Your uniform's ruined," Billy whispered, crouching down to look into Jessie's face, ignoring the battle sounds around them. He couldn't allow himself to think about the hole going plumb through Jessie, or that it meant death.

A reedy wail finally escaped Jessie's throat as he toppled forward on his face into the lush Virginia grasses at Manassas that day in '61. It was a day Billy would remember forever. From then on he would understand mortality, through four more terrible years of bloody warfare. Death was more than a pale body wrapped in a purple blanket buried below ground. It was an end to the sweetness of life; a thought Billy would consider again and again each time his duty required him to pull the trigger.

Leon Pickett halted a few feet away from Billy. The quiet inside the Pink Garter became absolute, like the stillness on a frosty winter morning when falling snowflakes made no measurable sound. Pickett passed a glance up and down Billy's frame, then he looked at the woman.

"Go upstairs," a rasping voice commanded, a dry sound like sand under a boot heel.

Ann nodded quickly, reaching into the top of her dress for the money Billy dropped inside. "I had . . . another gentleman," she stammered. Her hands were trembling.

Pickett eyed Billy again. "Find another woman," he said in the same rough manner.

Billy thought about the Walker Colt strapped to his right leg, the time it would take to pull it from its holster. He was no match for an experienced shootist with a pistol, but it went against his grain to let Pickett push him. "I already paid her for the room," he said, meeting Pickett's level gaze with a look of his own. Pickett had iron-gray eyes with black centers that revealed nothing—no fear, no emotion. He was tall, close to thirty or a little beyond, and he carried himself like a man who calculated every move.

"You ain't listenin'," Pickett said, a little softer and full of menace. "I told you to find another woman. This one's mine."

Billy forced a grin. "Not tonight she ain't. I told you I paid for her. Find yourself another girl."

Pickett's eyelids hooded. A muscle twitched in his right cheek. "Your fixin' to be proved dead wrong, cowboy. The whore ain't yours tonight. Clear out, before I run out of patience. A whore ain't worth dyin' for . . ."

"Here's your money back," the woman said, trying to hand Billy his silver, briefly interrupting Pickett's cold stare.

Billy brushed her hand away with his forearm, without taking his eyes from the gunman. "I paid my money," he said quietly, a strange calm keeping his nerves steady, holding his gun hand near the butt of the Walker.

"You're behavin' like a goddamn fool," Pickett hissed, his teeth clenched.

Billy knew everyone in the room was watching now. "I may be a fool, but the woman is mine for part of the night. Any man who thinks otherwise is liable to get himself killed."

For a fleeting moment Pickett regarded Billy silently, not moving a muscle or shifting his gaze. Then he said, "That's some mighty tough talk comin' from a common saddle tramp. You think you can kill me with that gun you're carryin' on your hip?"

He gave Pickett a slight nod. Billy had inherited his pa's temper and didn't take well to be being prodded. "If I have to. As to the part about bein' a saddle tramp, I reckon I won't take no offense. Not comin' from a backshooter who robs drunks in back alleys."

Now Pickett's stare turned to ice. "That's the same as you callin' me out, sayin' I'm a backshooter."

"Call it anything you want, mister. But this woman is mine until my money's spent."

The gunman's eyes fell to Billy's Colt. "You ain't no kind of shooter, cowboy. How come you're willin' to die fer a night with this whore?"

Again, Billy was aware of the calm holding him steady. He wondered if it might only be too much whiskey. "It ain't been decided just yet who's gonna die. But the plain truth is, I paid for the woman an' she's spendin' the next hour or so with me. It ain't nothin' personal. Just business. She took my money."

Pickett tensed one rope-like arm above his pistol. "Then I say it's time we got our business settled," he said, sounding as sure of himself as a man can be. "Go for that gun an' I'll blow a hole in you big enough to toss a tomcat through."

"Please, Leon!" Ann cried, offering him Billy's silver. "I don't want this money! Make him take it, but don't kill nobody."

Pickett ignored her, never once taking his eyes from Billy. "It ain't up to me now," he whispered hoarsely. "When he reaches fer that gun, I'm gonna kill him deader'n pig shit."

From some dark corner of his brain Billy summoned courage he didn't feel. "You can have the first pull," he said, like it did not make any difference. A few whispers could be heard around the Pink Garter after he made the remark.

Pickett seemed mildly amused. "You're either crazy, or one hell of a fast draw with that shootin' iron. But I'm willin' to find out, cowboy. Let's take it outside . . ." He was interrupted by the heavy clump of boots entering the drinking parlor.

Billy risked a quick glance at the door. Two men in vested suits and high crown hats walked into the place balancing shotguns in their hands. The older of the two wore a star pinned to the lapel of his dusty brown coat.

"What's the trouble in here?" a deep voice asked, although he knew what the trouble was, for he was staring at Billy and at Leon Pickett's back side.

Pickett glanced over his shoulder. "No trouble, Marshal. Just a little disagreement over a woman, is all."

"There'd better not be any gunplay, Leon. Been real quiet around here lately, since you been out of town. Let's keep it that way, or me an' my deputy will be forced to ask for your gun.'' The city marshal gave Billy a cursory examination. ''I don't recall seein' you here before, stranger. Mind if I ask your name?''

''Don't mind at all,'' Billy replied, relaxing the tension in his gun hand a bit. ''My name's Billy Blue. Can't say as I've had occasion to visit this place until now. A friend recommended it to me on the ride up from Waco. He told me the Pink Garter had the prettiest women in Fort Worth.''

The lawman was momentarily silent, like he had to think on what Billy said. ''Never heard the name before,'' he said finally, glancing over to his deputy with a question on his face.

The deputy shrugged. ''Me neither, Tom. We ain't got no Wanted circulars on a feller named Billy Blue that I recall.''

The marshal addressed both of them when he said, ''I want it understood that there won't be no killin' goin' on in this part of town, boys. If you got differences, settle 'em elsewhere. I ain't gonna warn the two of you but this once.''

''There's still the matter of the whore,'' Pickett said, with a look toward Ann, then Billy. ''This here's my woman when I'm in town an' damn near anybody will vouch fer that.''

Ann was nodding her head before Pickett finished. ''He's as right as rain, Marshal Lucas. I'm Leon's girl, only this cowboy paid me before Leon come in an' now he won't take his money back from me.''

Marshal Lucas frowned. ''Pardon me for speakin' so plain, ma'am, but you took Blue's money fair an' square, seems to me. I ain't no county judge, but I'd say the law is on Blue's side. A woman who sells herself has got an obligation to keep her word after she takes a feller's money.

Can't hardly see how you can change your mind without no reason . . ."

Pickett gave Ann a look that would have melted snow.

"I've got a reason," she said weakly, backing away a half step while color drained from her cheeks.

Before Ann could state whatever reason she had for changing her mind, an older woman in a pale green dress came to the top of the stairs overlooking the parlor. "What the hell's the trouble down there?" the woman barked, scowling, resting her hands on a pair of wide corseted hips.

Marshal Lucas turned to the stairwell. "Evenin', Belle," he said politely, touching the brim of his Stetson. "Two gents have got themselves in a disagreement over one of your gals. One paid his money first, an' now Leon wants the woman to hand the money back so's he can buck-jump her, I reckon. Looked like they was fixin' to have more'n just words over it."

Belle glared down from the railing, flame-red hair catching light from lanterns around the room. She saw Leon first, then she looked at Billy. "I won't tolerate any ruckus in my place," she said, watching Ann now. "I run a quiet establishment and I intend to keep it that way. The gentleman who paid first is the man who gets the girl first. It's a rule of my house."

Pickett took a step in Belle's direction. "You're liable to regret that, Belle," he snarled. "You know damn good an' well Ann is my woman when I'm in town."

Belle appeared unmoved by Pickett's threat. "Ann works for me and she'll do exactly what I tell her to do so long as she is one of my girls. Get that through your thick skull, Leon. You may have your bluff in on most of the menfolk in this town, but I don't bluff quite so easy. Ann goes upstairs with the cowboy at the bar." She turned to Marshal Lucas. "Tom, please escort Mr. Pickett outside. He may return when Ann is finished with her other gentleman caller.''

''It's your place, Belle,'' the marshal said, bowing slightly before he swung around to Pickett. ''You heard the lady, Leon. I want you out of here.''

Pickett had turned for the door, when suddenly he halted in mid stride, looking over his shoulder at Billy. ''I'll be lookin' you up sooner or later, cowboy,'' he promised. ''We got some unfinished business, you an' me.'' After saying that, he sauntered past Marshal Lucas and his deputy to go outside.

A murmur of hushed conversation spread through the drinkers and women around the room. Billy took a deep breath, noticing that the woman named Belle was still standing at the top of the stairs watching him.

Ann reached for his hand. ''Come upstairs,'' she whispered, ''before Leon changes his mind and comes back.''

He followed her to the stairway. The marshal and his deputy walked through the door. Billy's legs were a little unsteady as he took the steps two at a time. Whatever it was that had calmed him earlier while he faced Leon Pickett was gone now. A voice inside his head told him he would be seeing Pickett again before he hired-on with a cattle herd and got away from Fort Worth.

THREE

He drank deeply from a six-dollar bottle of bad whiskey he purchased after leaving Ann's room by the back stairs. Walking slowly down dark alleyways reeking of urine, behind saloons and gambling houses near the edge of the district, he listened to a mixture of raucous laughter and off-key music, the sounds of his boots in mud, the rattle of his spurs. The hour he spent with Ann seemed a waste now, after his seed was spent. He had two dollars and small change to his name, and what was far worse, a gunman of considerable ill reputation looking for him to settle accounts between them over a whore. Hardly what he'd had in mind when he rode up to Fort Worth to find work. All he had wanted was a sporting woman and enough whiskey so he could drop off to sleep at night.

Billy paused at a dark cross street to look both ways for sign of Leon Pickett, feeling like a hunted animal hiding out in the shadows. The courage he felt when Pickett braced him over the woman had vanished into thin air somehow. He could only judge it had been the product of a skull full of whiskey. Sober now, he was left to face the aftermath of his brazen challenge fully conscious of the possible consequences. He could be dead in a few hours if Pickett found him.

Finding the road empty, he crossed it as quietly as he could and hurried down an adjoining alley on the balls of his feet, with the neck of the bottle clenched tightly in his fist. His boots smelled of piss and rotted garbage, which was akin to the way he felt about himself right then. If only he had kept his big mouth shut when Pickett came to the Pink Garter . . .

He sighted the rooftop of the livery outlined against a black night sky and made a turn to fetch his horse and saddle. If he got out of Fort Worth before sunrise, there was a chance Pickett might forget the whole affair. Unlikely, perhaps, given that men like Pickett seldom backed down publicly. It was too harmful to a gunman's reputation to be slighted in front of an audience like the one at the Pink Garter. Word of such a thing would spread and soon Pickett's reputation would be tarnished, backing off in front of so many people the way he did, even though a pair of peace officers had been the ones to force him out of the place.

Circling a puddle of muddy ooze, Billy halted below an eave where shadows were the deepest to take a thirsty pull from the jug of whiskey to steady his nerves. He drank again when he saw how badly his hands were shaking. Listening to the night sounds around him, breathing the stench of the alley's offal heaps and latrine pits, he became so disgusted with himself that he shook his head. "I'd rather face the bastard an' die like a man," he muttered under his breath, not quite sure he truly believed what he just said. "It'd be better to die than hide like a goddamn chicken thief."

He replaced the cork in the neck of his bottle and stood a little straighter, until his backbone was ramrod stiff. In this fashion he marched out from under the eave, through the mud to the end of the alley, and rounded a corner. The stable was a short half block away. Stamping mud and urine from his boots and spur rowels, he continued down the dark road in a more dignified way to pick up his horse. Even though the street was deserted, he was feeling better about the way he looked now. He never considered himself a prideful man, but there were times when even a simple cowboy needed to hold his head up high.

The livery was deserted. A fact he'd been counting on since he had so little money to pay for the gelding's board bill. Six dollars was barely enough to feed himself for a couple of days, and only if he was careful about it. Slipping quietly into the hall of the barn, he edged down the rows of stalls until he found his branded bay and his saddle hanging on a fence rail. He took down the bridle and eased into the stall, making as little noise as possible. With just a little luck he would be out of town in less than an hour, seeking a trail hand's job among the crews assembling west of town for drives up the Chisholm. Some of the bigger herds were already pulling out for the Red River by now, he'd been told.

When his horse was saddled, he led it out of the barn and got mounted. Looking both ways, he elected to ride east until he was well clear of the city, hoping to avoid a possible run-in with Pickett. He took a final deep pull from the bottle and tucked it into his saddlebags. Foremen in charge of trail crews had a low regard for drunken cowboys. If he hoped to find a job, he knew he had better be cold sober asking for work on a cattle drive.

Trotting his bay through quiet residential sections of town, he thought about his narrow brush with death. Why had he been so quick to openly challenge a man like Pickett? Had he gone out of his mind completely? Or was the answer much simpler—too much in the way of liquid courage under his belt.

"It's a habit you need to break, ol' hoss," he told himself, reining his gelding north where houses were set farther apart at the outskirts of Fort Worth. Off to the northwest he could see open rangeland. Hoping there was a trail crew in need of a horse wrangler or a drag rider, the worst jobs on any drive, he kicked the bay to a short lope and rode toward gently rolling hills with high expectations for finding employment—and breakfast at any one of the chuck wagons he would encounter while he was looking.

Glancing over his shoulder, he found his backtrail clear of pursuit. Pickett was probably in the room with Ann now, having forgotten all about the ugly incident in the downstairs parlor a few hours earlier. Billy took a deep breath of fresh air and let it out slowly. Three or four months on a cow trail to Kansas was what he needed to freshen his outlook and put some badly needed money in his pocket. After a long, hard winter working day jobs around Waco he'd had enough of city life and fence building, or cutting firewood. All winter long he'd been wrestling with a dose of wanderlust, and with spring coming green to the prairies, it was too much to ask of any cowboy to stay put through an entire cow season, dreaming of the excitement on the Chisholm and all the attractions to be found in towns at trail's end, like Abilene or Dodge City. Never mind that there would be plenty of hardship to go around on the way to Kansas. Hardship was almost a way of life for a cowboy. After four years of shepherding groups of steers up the Chisholm, he'd grown accustomed to the river crossings, the cold, the heat, sleeping on hard ground. It was quite simply a part of the job, but it was a job with more freedom than any work he had ever known.

Roughly four miles north and a little west of town he came upon the first sleeping herd spread out across a winding creek bottom. Night riders rode slow circles in opposite directions around hundreds of resting longhorns, singing in creaky voices or whistling to lull the steers into a quiet mood. Longhorns were the most fractious beasts on earth when something riled them up, and any experienced cow hand knew that getting them bedded down and keeping them there was the key to an uneventful evening for a cattle crew. Stampedes were all too common under the very best of circumstances, and it fell to night riders to prevent such an occurrence whenever possible. Thus Billy rode toward the sleeping herd cautiously, staying wide of downed steers to angle for the chuck wagon and a glowing fire close by, where coffee was on all night for men riding herd in the dark. When he was a polite distance away, he would announce himself to the camp cook and ask permission to ride to the fire, necessary cowboy etiquette that would keep him from being shot out of the saddle, or at the very least kept at gunpoint until his identity was made known.

Slowing his horse to a walk, he made for the wagon sheet on tent poles covering the chuck box and worktable where the cook prepared meals. He saw a smoke-blackened coffeepot hanging on an iron rod above dying embers in a firepit, and when the wind was just right, he caught scent of Arbuckle's. When he was in hailing distance, he reined down on the bay and said, "Halloo the fire!" in a reasonably loud voice, still quiet enough not to spook a nervous bunch of Mexican steers.

A sleeping form stirred underneath the chuck wagon, then a blanket was tossed aside and a man sat up. "Who's callin'?" an unhappy voice asked, a voice still thick with slumber.

"The name's Billy Blue an' I'm lookin' for work with a herd headed to Kansas. Has your bossman got any spots open with this outfit?"

A silence followed, probably because the man had been sound asleep and required a moment or two to clear his head. "Nary a one that I recall, cowboy, but yer welcome to ride in an' have a cup of sludge if you've a mind to whilst I think about it a bit more. Seems there was another outfit huntin' a feller or two, but it slips my mind jest now. Kinda early to be askin' a man to think, ain't it?"

"Sorry. Can't afford no timepiece so I was only guessin' at the hour. I figured dawn can't be too far off." He urged the bay closer to the chuck wagon on a tight rein while the cook was crawling out from under the wagon bed. Dressed in worn longjohns with holes in the knees and elbows, whiskers decorating his chin, the cook sauntered over to a washtub and took a clean tin cup from the drying rack as Billy rode to the fire. Lighting a tiny lantern, the man glanced at his pocket watch, scowling.

"You sure as hell ain't no judge of time, son," the old man said gruffly, watching Billy dismount. "It ain't but four in the mornin', too goddamn early to be prospectin' fer any work."

"I said I was sorry. It was a long ride up from Waco an' I lost track of time, I reckon." He ground-hitched the bay and went over for the cup, grinning to help soften his early arrival.

"Help yerself. It's liable to be thick as buffalo taller by now, but it's all I got."

"I'm obliged. By the way, what's the name of this outfit?"

"Taylor," the cook replied, appraising Billy more carefully in the light from the lantern. "The ranch lies just south of San Antone by a day's ride. We got ourselves a full crew, but you kin ask our ramrod soon as he gits up if he knows anybody lookin' fer a trail hand."

"Who's the foreman?" Billy asked, pouring thick black coffee that was, as the cook had predicted, mighty close to sludge.

"Cal Taylor. He's asleep over yonder an' I'd sooner wake up a grizzly than ask him to leave his bedroll afore he's ready. I can rustle up some of last night's biscuits, if'n yer hungry."

"I could eat," he said, sipping the scalding coffee carefully to avoid burning his mouth. "Most anything will do . . ."

A horse and rider came toward the fire, a cowboy slumped over his saddle horn like his belly hurt. "Got any soda, Cookie?" a young voice asked from the darkness. "I drank so damn much of that rotgut last night that I swear I'm gonna die." A slender boy dropped from his saddle to the ground before he took a closer look at Billy. "Howdy, stranger. I seen you someplace before, ain't I?"

Billy grinned, saying, "Not to my recollection, but I never was known for a long memory."

The boy continued to examine Billy's face. "I remember you now," he said, a trace of excitement in it. "You was the gent who stood up to Leon Pickett at the Pink Garter last night. Told him to go fer his gun if he took the notion. It was over that real pretty yellow-haired gal, if I ain't mistaken."

A knot twisted in Billy's stomach. The last thing he wanted was to be recognized by anyone who knew Pickett and saw what had happened between them. "You must be mistaken," he said quickly. "I wasn't at the Pink Garter last night. Must be somebody who looks a little bit like me, maybe."

"No sir," the cowboy stated emphatically. "It was you sure as snuff makes spit. You tol' Pickett he could have the first pull with a gun. I was standin' just down the bar a ways an' I heard the whole thing real clear. Saw it was you, mister. You told that lawman yer name was Blue. Billy Blue . . ."

It was pointless to deny it now, Billy decided. "Maybe it was the Pink Garter I was in. Just then I couldn't recall the name of the place. There wasn't much to it, really. The feller in the topcoat tried to run his bluff on me an' I wouldn't have any part of it, that's all.''

The young cowboy edged closer to Billy, and there was a look of wonderment on his face when he said, ''That gent wasn't runnin' no bluff, mister. That was none other than Leon Pickett hisself, one of the worst badmen in this part of the state. You got it figured wrong if you thought Leon Pickett was bluffin'. I seen him gun down Boyd Pierce last year over in Brownwood. Pierce never got his pistol clear of leather before Leon shot him stone-cold dead through the heart. Boyd Pierce was said to be mighty fast with a six-gun, but he never stood no kind of chance at all goin' up against the likes of Leon.''

''That so?'' Billy asked. It seemed he remembered hearing a thing or two about Pierce being a gunfighter. Was Pickett truly as good with a gun as the young cowboy said? Billy noticed that the cook and the night rider were staring at his holstered pistol just then. He tried to think of something to say that would put the business with Pickett to rest. ''There wasn't all that much to it, like I said before. It was over a saloon whore . . .''

Their conversation brought another cowboy from his bedroll near the remuda. A lanky figure put on his boots and came over to the fire. ''Mornin', boys,'' he said, eyeing Billy. ''I heard talk. Anything wrong?''

The cook wagged his head. ''Nothin', Boss, jest this feller who rode up lookin' fer a job. This here's Billy Blue. Meet the foreman of this outfit, Cal Taylor.''

Billy shook hands with Taylor. ''Sorry I woke everybody up. I didn't know it was so early.''

Taylor shrugged. ''We've got a full crew, but the Burnet outfit is lookin' for a horse wrangler. See Burke Burnet over at the next herd west of us, if you've a hankerin' to wrangle horses up to Kansas.''

''I'm not real particular about the work,'' Billy replied.

"See ol' Burke right after first light, an' you can tell him I sent you over."

Billy digested this news with a feeling of relief. It was beginning to look like he'd have a job this spring after all, so long as he got away from Fort Worth without any bullet holes in his hide. Glancing up at the stars, he wondered if his string of bad luck was about to change for the better.

FOUR

A ball of yellow light creeping over the horizon announced the arrival of dawn as Billy rode toward a smoky breakfast fire near the edge of a post oak forest northwest of the Taylor herd. Following directions given by Cal and the cook, he found a vast herd of longhorns spread along the winding, tree-lined banks of a narrow stream where Burke Burnet had assembled one of the largest bunches of cattle to start up the Chisholm that spring, over five thousand head of unruly Mexican steers known for their refusal to develop a gentle trail disposition. Thus it was that Burnet needed a sizable remuda, according to Cal, in order to keep fresh horses under his men while they attempted to move Mexican-bred steers and keep them collected. Billy knew a thing or two about driving Mexican cattle—it was a difficult proposition at best, requiring that cowboys continually be on the lookout for any sign that a stampede was in the making. For when Mexican cows bolted and ran, it was a sight no one ever forgot, a mass of beef on the hoof moving in whatever direction it wanted at top speed, with few chances of being forced to a halt until the cows ran themselves out.

As Billy trotted his bay closer to the Burnet camp, he gave things a cursory inspection. The outfit sported a new Studebaker wagon and a remuda of sleek, fat cow horses, and by the general look of what he could see from a distance, it appeared to be a good bunch of men to go up a cattle trail with. Bigger outfits made arrangements for better food, better horses, and enough men on a crew to allow a few extra hours of sleep after a stint riding night herd. While the pay was usually the same, experienced drovers sought work with big herds ramrodded by foremen with a few years under their belt pushing cattle. Cowboying was one profession where knowledge was more valuable than a strong back and willing hands. Know-how kept men from drowning at swollen rivers or being trampled when a herd went on the run. And it was this seasoning to adversity on a cow trail Billy could offer the foreman of the Burnet herd. He'd been up the Chisholm before and knew most of its secrets.

A group of cowboys watched him ride toward the fire, and he knew they were sizing him up, judging him by the way he sat his saddle, the way he handled a horse. Men who earned a living from the hurricane deck of a cow pony were often harsh critics of their contemporaries when it came to horsemanship, or skill with a rope while in the saddle. First impressions often lasted for the duration of a drive, and with this in mind, Billy sat his bay like the veteran he was, making sure he made no greenhorn moves while the others were observing him ride.

He noticed that one member of the crew was grinning. "Is that you, Billy?" the cowboy shouted, pulling off a flop-brim hat to show more of his face.

Billy didn't recognize him, slowing his horse to get a good look at the man who called his name. The voice sounded vaguely familiar, he thought. Riding closer, he could make out a deeply tanned face and little else in the pale morning light. When he was near enough that shouting wasn't necessary, he asked, "Who are you?" of the stranger.

"It's me, Asa!" the cowboy replied cheerfully, leaving the fire to meet Billy before he got to the chuck wagon. "Have you gotten so old that you need spectacles, pardner?"

Billy abruptly reined his horse to a stop. "Can't be you, ol' hoss. Asa Carter stayed in Tennessee . . ."

"Like hell he did. I stayed almost a year, but I got this powerful itch to see Texas again." Asa hurried over to the bay while Billy was dismounting. He stuck out a hand, and he was grinning from ear to ear when they shook.

"You look older," Billy said, thinking maybe he did, too. It had been six or seven years since they'd seen each other. When the war ended, Asa went to see a girl near Memphis he met while he was recovering from a wound in his thigh at a field hospital. He hadn't come back to Waco since.

"Hell, we're both gettin' older, Billy. Come over to the fire an' meet the rest of the boys. What brings you out this way?"

Still surprised at meeting his friend from the war, Billy took a moment to answer. "Lookin' for work goin' up the trail, same as you, I reckon. I was told this outfit needed a wrangler when I asked some cowboys with the Taylor herd east of here."

Leading the way to the chuck wagon on deeply bowed legs, Asa replied, "I'll introduce you to the boss an' give him my best recommendation. It'll be like old times . . ."

Billy nodded. "I'd be obliged if you put a word in for me with the bossman. As to those old times, I'd just as soon forget most of 'em. I still dream about Jessie every now an' then."

Asa escorted him to a semicircle of cowboys gathered

near the cooking fire eating from tin plates. The smell of food made his belly growl.

"Boys," Asa began, "this here's an old pard of mine from down in Waco. Meet Billy Blue. Billy, this here's the crew for Burke Burnet. Yonder's Dutch, Pete, Sonny, Little Luke, Crawfish Thompson, Sam, Ike, an' Jimmie Dale. Billy's interested in the wranglin' job an' I aim to recommend him."

They all exchanged polite nods. "Howdy, men," Billy said, as he cast a sideways glance at the coffeepot and a skillet of eggs and bacon. "I know my way around a horse reasonable well an' I'd do my best to see that you're kept well mounted."

The cowboy called Crawfish shrugged and said, "If Asa says you kin do the work, that'll be good enough fer me. Same goes fer the rest of us, I reckon."

Another chorus of silent nods went around the group. Asa pointed to a three-sided tent close to the stream. "Yonder's the boss's headquarters, Billy. Grab yerself a plate of that grub an' then we'll go down an' talk to Mr. Burnet."

Billy ground-hitched his bay and ambled over to the back of the chuck wagon to pick up a plate and a cup. "I'm grateful for the feed bag," he said. "It'll be nice, knowin' I'll be able to eat regular for the next three or four months."

By the looks the other men gave him, he knew they understood.

The heavy chuck wagon bounced and jolted over uneven prairie on the way to Fort Worth to pick up supplies. Asa rode beside Billy behind the wagon as they talked about the war, and the years afterward. Billy had been given the wrangler's job at thirty a month and found after meeting Burke Burnet. The herd was due to pull out for Indian Territory tomorrow morning and the wagon was being sent to town to pick up supplies. Billy was to purchase whatever he needed in the way of horseshoes and rope for the remuda. Asa got permission to ride along to help load supplies in the wagon, and so they could catch up on old times. Billy felt good about his new employment. He liked Burnet, a burly man with honest eyes and a ruddy complexion, and the crew members he met after breakfast looked to be dependable. Overall, his prospects for the future had improved greatly since yesterday.

Asa had been talking about his recovery in Memphis and his short courtship with the young nurse. "She wasn't all that keen on me bein' a cowboy," he remembered, gazing off at the horizon. "When I said I was aimin' to head back to Texas to hire on at a ranch, she didn't cotton to the notion. After a bit I decided a woman wasn't worth givin' up everything for, so I saddled up my horse an' rode fer Texas. Got as far as the Burnet Ranch when I was offered a job, so it was where I stayed. Been with 'em ever since '69, Billy. Happy as a pig in the mud, most times."

"Sounds like you found yourself a home, Asa. I can't say I was all that lucky. Been sorta driftin' from place to place, had lots of bad jobs that didn't pay much, or the work wasn't dignified enough to suit me. Things have been kinda rough around Waco since the war."

"Leastways we made it through," Asa offered thoughtfully, a frown wrinkling his sun-darkened face. "There was a God's plenty who didn't, like Jessie Small. I got a hole in my leg, but that don't seem all that bad beside what happened to him."

Billy didn't want to remember Jessie—there had been enough nights when the memory of Jessie's death kept him from sleeping. "We were both mighty lucky," he said, sighting the skyline of Fort Worth in the distance, "and I'd say we're even luckier to have found each other like this, by pure accident."

"I'd call it the work of Lady Luck," Asa said. "It's like drawin' to an inside straight in a poker game. It don't happen all that often, but when it does, it sure as hell is a wonderment to behold."

The wagon creaked and clattered over a rocky hill to begin a gentle grade toward the outskirts of Fort Worth. Dust rose from the wheels and the horses' hooves until a stiff March wind swept it away in swirling clouds.

Just then, when Billy looked at the town, he felt a stirring behind his belt buckle, hoping that Leon Pickett wouldn't be near the outfitters store where they took on supplies. Until now he'd all but forgotten about the incident with Pickett. Seeing Fort Worth was an unwanted reminder of his brush with the notorious gunman.

"You ever hear of a gent by the name Leon Pickett?" he asked when the wagon team broke into a trot down the long slope to the road leading into town, noise from the axles and springs making it hard to hear his voice unless he shouted.

Asa gave him a worried look. "Hell yes I have, an' so has damn near everybody else who frequents the cribs and saloons in Hell's back pastures. How come you to ask?"

"Seems I had me a little run-in with him last night over a whore at the Pink Garter. I didn't know his reputation, so I let my tongue wag too much, maybe."

"Holy shit, Billy! You hadn't oughta get crossways with no owlhoot like Pickett. He's as cold as a blue norther crossin' the Panhandle. Fast as greased lightnin' with a gun an' he ain't got no soft spot in his heart for no man. Even the law in Fort Worth is scared to crowd him when he's in town. He's one ornery bastard. Mean as a two-headed rattlesnake. If you had a run-in with him, you're damn lucky to be alive this mornin' . . ."

This wasn't the sort of news Billy wanted, that Pickett

was as bad as his reputation made him out to be. "Maybe he's forgot about it by now."

"It'd be my guess that if he aimed to kill you he'd have done it last night."

"A couple of lawmen were there to put a stop to it, Marshal Tom Lucas and his deputy. They were carryin' shotguns an' it was them who headed it off by ordering Pickett out of the place when the trouble started."

Asa wagged his head doubtfully. "Maybe you hadn't oughta ride in with us just now, Billy. Me an' Crawfish can pick up the supplies you need. If Pickett was to hear that you was still in town, he might get a hump in his back an' come lookin' for you."

Billy's jaw clenched a little. The sons of Nathaniel Blue had been taught never to run away from a fight. "I've got a bit too much pride for that, pardner. I'll face up to what I did if he pushes it."

By the look on Asa's face, he was set to vote against that notion. "You don't look like you wintered all that good to me, an' this job with Mr. Burnet could get you back on your feed by the time we make payday. But in order for you to be there to get that pay envelope, you're gonna have to be in one piece. It makes more sense to give Pickett a wide berth, if you ask me."

"I won't be lookin' for any trouble, just horseshoe nails and some spools of rope, a few sets of new iron for the slick-shod geldings. Pickett ain't likely to be hangin' around close to an outfitters place this time of day."

"All the same, Billy boy, I'd feel some better if you didn't go into town."

Billy grinned over his old friend's concern. "You're still a worrier, Corporal Carter. You was worried we'd never get out of Nashville with our skins, but we fooled them Yanks."

At that, Asa chuckled. "That's about as close as I ever

aim to come to gettin' myself killed again. We damn near didn't make it out before they overrun us that time." He looked at Billy as soon as he said it. "You an' me have been all the way to hell an' back together. It's sure as hell good to see you again. I'd plumb given up on the idea of settin' eyes on you this side of them pearly gates. Wish you'd listen to my advice an' stay out of town until we get this wagon loaded."

They struck the road leading into Fort Worth's west side as Billy was preparing his final remarks on the subject. "I won't let anybody run me out of a town, pardner. This Pickett feller can't be all that tough. Now, leave it be, and let's look for the prettiest gal we can find to say our howdy-dos before we hit that long trail to Abilene. It's gonna be a spell before we see any womenfolk, and I figure we oughta have a pretty one to remember on all those lonesome nights ridin' herd around a bunch of steers."

Asa didn't say any more, but he was still worried as they followed the wagon into Fort Worth. He rode beside Billy, but as they passed the first of many storefronts on the way to the central business district, he paid close attention to everyone they saw on the boardwalks and porches lining the street.

Billy began exercising his own brand of caution, removing a thin rawhide hammer thong from the thumb piece of his Walker Colt .44. Down in his gut he wanted a drink of whiskey to steady his nerves, but with a new job hanging in the balance he wasn't going to let old habits cost him a spot on the Burnet Ranch payroll.

They sighted White's Outfitters at a fork in the road near the central stockyards. Billy was sure a gunman the likes of Pickett wouldn't be out and about at this early hour in a place where cattle trading was the prime business activity. It was a quarter mile or more to the edge of Hell's Half

Acre, and he was certain that was where Pickett spent the night, in the room with Ann above the Pink Garter. Asa had gotten himself all worked up into a nervous stew over nothing.

FIVE

The outfitter's shelves displayed everything imaginable in neat rows running the length of an old whitewashed building. Wonderful smells of indigo, scented soap, and peppermint made Billy remember his early childhood. His first visit to the Brazos Valley Mercantile on Elm Street in Waco had been like entering a world of dreams.

Clutching his mother's skirt at that mercantile, Billy had discovered his first taste of flavors like root beer, licorice, chocolate, wintergreen, and best of all, peppermint sticks. Lumps of brown sugar, the simplest of treats, melted on his tongue for the first time, and from then on the store would be the most special place on earth to him. When he was nine years old, his first pair of shoes came from those same store shelves, leather high-top work shoes with latigo laces made slippery with Neatsfoot oil. Shoes that carried him merrily across grass burrs and goathead sticker patches that once crippled him like a road-foundered horse. He had never been prouder of anything than he'd been of that first pair of work shoes, and when his feet finally outgrew them, he felt a touch of sorrow handing them down to his younger brother, Robert James. Even when they were so badly worn they couldn't be resoled by a cobbler again, he couldn't bring himself to see them thrown away. He'd kept them underneath his bed for years, until he went away to war at age sixteen, and had there been room in his rucksack, he might have taken them along as a keepsake, or a good luck charm. Now, as he stood inside White's Outfitters breathing in the smells, his gaze wandered to the racks of boots and shoes. If a dose of good fortune brought him any extra money at the end of the trail, he vowed to buy himself a new pair of stovepipe boots this year.

Crawfish was giving a store clerk his order for staples as Billy sauntered past the counter to locate horseshoes, nails, and rope. Part of a wrangler's job was seeing to any blacksmithing chores needed by the crew. Shoeing a green-broke horse was sometimes the most dangerous part of a wrangler's work, since a colt could kick hard enough to cripple a man for life if he was not extra careful around its rear legs. The only thing worse than a horse's kick was a mule's. Mules had been known to kill careless men with a well-aimed hoof, and they were unpredictable as to when they would kick. Harnessing a team of mules to a wagon was as dangerous as shoeing one, for when the beasts felt anything touch their back legs they were inclined to kick it to oblivion if they could. Martha Blue claimed that Nathaniel Blue's skull would surely have been crushed by the kicking his mule gave him, had he not been born with extra thick head bones. She also said it was a miracle, an act by the hand of God, sparing Nathaniel's life. Billy and his younger brothers were more inclined to view the miracle as a curse, since their regular whippings resumed two short weeks afterward.

Billy found a carton of horseshoe nails and a box of iron shoe blanks that could be heated and hammered to any size. He added two spools of sisal rope to his purchases and carried them to the front of the store.

"This stuff gits charged to us, too," Crawfish said, with a nod toward the supplies Billy piled near the front door.

"Anything Burke wants is okay by me," the clerk remarked as he made a notation on the bill of goods before him.

Billy ambled over to the candy jars, recalling his youth so vividly that his mouth watered. He reached into a pocket of his faded denims and found cent pieces for two sticks of peppermint candy, one for himself and one for Asa. Asa was standing outside keeping watch over the mule team and their horses when Billy came out with the red-and-white candy sticks.

"Here's somethin for your sweet tooth," Billy said, offering Asa a peppermint.

Asa grinned. "We'd have traded our own souls fer a stick of this that summer in Virginia when the rations run out."

"Our rations were always running out," Billy remembered, a bite of candy melting on his tongue. "Seems like we ran out of just about everything back then. Ran out of courage a few times, too. Plenty of times. Only man I ever saw who never ran out of guts was Jessie. He run straight at those Yanks like a lead ball couldn't hurt him none at all."

Asa's face darkened. "You're wrong about one thing," he said quietly. "Jessie never had time to grow to be a man. He was just a kid, same as us, when they shot him down."

Billy swallowed sweet peppermint juice and nodded his head in agreement, wishing he hadn't remembered Jessie right then. "If the truth got told, there was plenty of boys younger'n us who died in that war." Gazing across the rooftops of Fort Worth, his mind drifted back for a time to battles in Virginia and Tennessee and northern Georgia. Franklin, Tennessee, had been the worst, the hardest to think about. Eight thousand Confederates lost their lives there in three bloody days of fighting. "It ain't good for a man to spend too much time rememberin' it, Asa. Best we forget about it, if we can."

Asa's teeth ground away at a piece of candy until he could speak. "I can't forget about it. 'Specially at night. I wake up soakin' wet with the recollection real plain inside my head . . ."

"So do I," Billy whispered. "Sometimes I can't sleep a wink for thinkin' about it. Wish it'd go away, but it won't."

"I don't dream about it near so often the last year or so," Asa confided. "Maybe it goes away over time . . ."

"Sure wish it would," Billy added, as the clerk and Crawfish came out of the store with their arms loaded down carrying boxes of provisions. "Let's lend these gents a hand so we can say we earned our keep."

They fell in to help load the wagon. A mid-morning sun rose above the street, warming them to a sweat before their job was finished. Neither Billy nor Asa said much of anything after the discussion about war. Had it not been for the presence of others right then, Billy would have opted for a few generous swallows from his bottle of whiskey to help drive away unwanted memories.

Crawfish lashed down the side curtains when the loading was finished. A southerly breeze fluttered the wagon sheet between its bows. Now and then a carriage or a buckboard passed by them, and as the morning wore away, there were more people walking past the store. An occasional bunch of cowboys rode toward the cattle pens. Some looked longingly at store windows where new boots with fancy stitched tops were displayed. Billy understood the wishful looks on their faces. New boots would always remind him of that first pair of shoes he got, the feel of new leather in his hands and the smell of oil. When he looked down at his run-over boots now, it made him feel a little sad that he couldn't afford to buy himself replacements, not even half soles. Being poor was the worst condition on earth, he decided.

His eyes wandered to the end of the street, where a man in a black coat and hat rounded a corner near the shipping corrals. A sleek dappled gray horse carried its rider toward the outfitter's at a jog trot—there was something about the man that made Billy take a closer look. Then he felt his heart skip a beat. He knew the rider's identity.

"Yonder's Pickett," he said evenly, while Asa was helping to tie a rope around a barrel of flour. Billy pushed away from the front wall of the store where he'd been leaning, removing the bit of latigo cord from the hammer of his Walker.

"It's him!" Asa cried, turning to look at Billy. "I knowed all along you should have stayed clear of town . . ."

"That's Leon Pickett, all right," Crawfish muttered, moving a cud of chewing tobacco to the other cheek. "Won't be nothin' but misery followin' him tonight, wherever that buzzard decides to roost. How come you act so riled up over him, Asa?"

Asa was watching Billy's face. "Because him an' my pardner got crossways over a woman last night. Go back inside the store, Billy," he pleaded softly. "Maybe that way he won't see you and make a fuss."

"I won't run from him," Billy said, watching Pickett ride up the street alone. "He's just one man."

"Don't be a fool, Billy!"

Billy walked to the edge of the front porch, ignoring what Asa said, his full attention focused on Pickett now. The dappled gray would pass by White's store in a moment. Would Pickett be the kind to forget about the incident over Ann? Experience was against it.

"We ain't got any guns," Asa said, spreading his palms

in a helpless gesture. ''You'll be on your own if he decides to call you out . . .''

Billy wasn't listening. He hadn't expected any help from Asa or Crawfish. If Pickett called for a duel, it would be just between the two of them.

Pickett saw him now, reining his horse to come closer to the porch where Billy stood. Then, at about fifty paces, he brought his gray to a sudden stop.

''Here it comes,'' Billy whispered to himself, his right hand near the butt of his Colt, fingers curled. He knew instinctively that Pickett would challenge him to a contest at the draw.

The gunman sat quietly for a moment, shoulders rounded, one elbow resting on his saddle horn. There was no expression on his face that Billy could see, only a cold, unwavering stare from the shadow below his hat brim.

Billy returned the look, frozen in place. His heart began to hammer wildly. Once again he thought about death. During the war there had been so many times when he was sure he was at death's door, only to survive. Something his pa used to say echoed through his thoughts . . . A brave man only dies once, while a coward dies a thousand times. Jessie Small had died bravely. Billy knew he could never equal Jessie's courage, but did that make him a coward?

''I've been lookin' for you,'' Pickett said, the sound of his voice like a grate on Billy's nerves. ''Somebody told me you'd hightailed it out of town.''

From the corner of his eye Billy saw Asa creep toward the front of the chuck wagon, staying behind it. ''That somebody was wrong,'' he said, rocking back on his boot heels just a little to keep his knees from trembling. ''I'm right here. No need to look any longer . . .''

''Funny,'' Pickett remarked, without grinning. ''I had you pegged for a yellow bastard. Figured it was whiskey doin' all that big talkin' last night.''

"I'd had a few. But it was me doin' the talking. I ain't yellow, an' I sure as hell ain't no bastard, either. If you've got business with me, let's get it settled."

The gunman nodded and swung down from his horse, keeping a close eye on Billy's gun hand. He dropped his reins and stepped away from his dappled gray gelding. The horse wandered off with its reins dragging through powdery dust between wagon ruts. A few paces closer and then Pickett stopped, spreading his feet apart. "We got unfinished business, you an' me. You called me a backshooter in front of everybody at Belle's. That don't leave me no choice but to kill you from the front side, to prove you was wrong."

Again, the sudden dryness occurring in his mouth. "You make it sound like killin' me is gonna be easy."

A silence. Pickett's eyelids narrowed. "I'm guessin' it'll be real easy, cowboy. You'll be too slow."

"Maybe. The way to find out is make a grab for that six-gun you're carryin'. If I'm slow, you get the first shot. But I'll promise you this . . . I won't miss at close range. You had better make damn sure your aim is good. Mine is."

Another hesitation before Pickett spoke. "You sound mighty sure of yourself. Of your aim."

"I got plenty of practice at Bull Run and Nashville, a few other places. Four years of learnin' how to hit what I aim at."

Pedestrians ambling along the boardwalks stopped when they saw Pickett standing in the middle of the road with his hand poised near his gun. A buggy driven by an older woman slowed and came to a halt down the street. Dust settled around the wheels.

"Enough talk," Pickett snarled, and he had hunkered down, when another voice sounded from the front of the chuck wagon.

"Reach fer that gun an' I'll blow your goddamn head off!"

The voice was Asa's, and when Billy looked that way he saw twin shotgun barrels aimed from a spot near the wagon seat.

Pickett was watching Asa now, undecided. He took a half step backward, raising his hands for everyone to see. "You got the drop on me, cowboy. Don't squeeze that trigger too damn hard . . ."

"Git on that gray an' don't look back!" Asa shouted. "If I can't see them hands, I swear I'll shoot!"

Pickett backed farther away, keeping his palms lifted until he made a slow turn for his horse. With both hands in plain sight while looking over his shoulder at Asa, he walked to the dappled gray and climbed into his saddle. He glanced back to the porch where Billy stood, like he meant to say something. Then he apparently thought better of it and reined down the street in a cloud of dust.

Billy's legs felt weak. He took a deep breath and let it out slowly when Pickett rode out of sight behind a building near the cattle pens.

Crawfish Thompson was shaking his head. "You hadn't oughta done that, Asa. You bought into troubles that weren't no part of your own."

Asa came from the front of the chuck wagon with the shotgun dangling at his side. "I took a side with my pardner, Crawfish," he said, glancing up at Billy. "Won't make no apology for it."

"I'm grateful," Billy told Asa quietly, "but you needn't have done it."

Asa shrugged and grinned halfheartedly. "Wasn't no choice but to fetch this scattergun from under the seat when it looked like you was headed fer a one-sided fight. Good thing I remembered Crawfish kept his huntin' gun under that seat . . ."

A part of Billy wanted to say that he hadn't needed any help facing the gunfighter. Twice now, he'd come to the brink with Pickett and fate had kept them from finding out who was faster with a gun.

He took another breath of fresh air. "I'm obliged" was all he could think of to tell Asa just then. "Let's get our supplies out to the herd or we'll be late gettin' 'em started for Kansas."

SIX

On the ride back to join the herd, Billy was in a somber mood remembering his second confrontation with Leon Pickett. He owed Asa his life, perhaps, although there had been something about it that made him regret not having to face the gunman's challenge, a nagging doubt about how he'd done it with the help of a friend. A test of sorts had come his way and he'd avoided it twice by sheer luck. He tried to sort through it in his mind and couldn't come up with answers that made any sense. He was alive. So why was he troubled?

"You seem kinda quiet, Billy." Concern furrowed Asa's brow as he rode beside him. "You still thinkin' about how close you come to gettin' yourself killed?"

"I'm not so all-fired sure he'd have killed me, Asa. I sure can't lay no claim to bein' a shootist, but things still haven't been settled between the two of us. Next time we meet I'll have to face it all over again. It sticks in my craw like sand when a feller pushes me like that. Just now, I was thinkin' how I wish it was over, one way or another."

"You mean you'd just as soon be dead?"

That was the hard part, putting it into words why he felt

it wouldn't have ended that way. "Maybe he ain't as fast as everybody thinks. Or maybe his aim ain't so good. To tell the truth I was scared, but not so scared that I'd have backed down when it was time to reach for guns. A man has to face up to things every once in a while, like findin' out who he really is, if he's got a yellow streak." He stared thoughtfully at the rear of the wagon jolting over rough ground in front of them. "I'd made up my mind that I was gonna find out how I stacked up against him. I had a feelin' it was gonna turn out all right. It's hard to explain."

"Hell, Billy, you proved you didn't have no yellow streak in the war. Everybody in Company C knowed how brave you was. That time they rushed us in the snow at Nashville . . . you stayed put in that old barn an' kept shootin' whilst most of the others was set to run for the woods. But it's one thing to be brave an' all, an' it's another to be plumb crazy. Drawin' a gun against a gent the likes of Leon Pickett don't make any sense for a cowboy. He made a big name for himself by bein' fast. I hear tell he's shot eight or nine men, maybe more."

The feeling lingered that things would have worked out for him, but it was pointless to argue over it with Asa. Asa had done more than most by risking his neck for a friend. He owed him a favor, not more argument. "It took guts to do what you did and I'll always be grateful. You coulda stayed hid behind that wagon until one of us got shot down. If someone had asked me yesterday, I'd have said I never figured to see Asa Carter again. Just this mornin' you up an' hand me a job goin' to Kansas an' save my skin from a bullet hole. Hard for a man to have a better friend than you, ol' hoss."

Asa grinned. "It was Lady Luck, pardner. She brung you my way sure as Hell gets hot. We're gonna have ourselves one fine time on that cattle road to Abilene. An' when we get there, we'll dance with every pretty gal there is an' drink the town plumb dry of whiskey.''

Billy quickly forgot about this morning's events and put his mind on the drive to Kansas Territory. ''I had this bad itch all winter long to ride the Chisholm again. Makes it twice as good to ride it with you this year. Like you say, we'll drink up all the whiskey in Abilene an' buck-jump every pretty woman in town till the sun comes up. I can't hardly wait to get there . . .''

''You ever get serious about a woman, Billy?''

''Can't say as I ever have, really. I've been flat broke most every day of my life, an' that condition tends to make a man forget about decent womenfolk. I've had my share of saloon gals over the years, but nary a one worth thinkin' twice about. Way back when I was a kid, I got silly over a girl named Sallie Mae Barnes, but she took a likin' to Warren Cobb soon as she found out my family was dirt poor. Most women aint' got much use for a poor man . . .''

Asa let the subject drop, and for that Billy was glad.

Off in the distance they could see the back of the Burnet herd crawling like horned ants over rolling prairie hills. This would be like other drives, full of hardship, long hours spent in a saddle, sleepless nights when the cows were jittery. But with the misery there would be plenty of the freedom Billy prized so greatly, riding beneath open skies, footloose on the back of a cow pony in open country where there were no fences. He would be at peace with himself, and there was no way to place a value on that sort of thing.

An hour later they caught up with the rear of the herd, and Billy swung off to take charge of the remuda trailing along in the steers' dust. A young cowpoke by the name of Jimmie Dale had been assigned to move the horses until Billy got back, and when he saw Billy he waved a friendly greeting and spurred off to ride drag behind the longhorns.

Asa followed the chuck wagon toward the front of the herd, leaving Billy to push the riding stock.

Billy gave the remuda a rough head count—better than fifty good geldings and four reserve mules, for the wagon and for dragging logs to the rivers so their chuck and gear could be floated across deep spots. Settling back against the cantle, he allowed himself to feel contentment for the first time in many months. A drive was under way and he was signed on with a top outfit. Now he was sure his fortune had begun to change for the better. The Burnet Ranch crew seemed like good company, mostly experienced men who wouldn't need coddling. Working a remuda for a bunch of seasoned cowboys was almost pleasurable, hardly like work at all.

Gazing north, he watched the herd move snake-like across a range of low hills, grazing as they went. A longhorn was remarkable in this regard, for it could put on weight as it was being moved to market, as long as the grass was good and there was water. It was a sight to see—thousands of animals moving the same direction, five- or six-foot horn spreads glistening in the sun. Billy could hear the bawling that set in when longhorns called to each other for no apparent reason. A cowboy got used to the cattle calls and after a while didn't notice it all that much, until the cows fell silent at night bedding down. Then the quiet seemed almost eerie, like the calm before a storm, which it was sometimes if a herd got spooked and went on a nighttime stampede.

Later that afternoon, while Billy was urging slower horses up with the rest of the bunch, he spotted a rider coming his way from the direction of the herd. He soon recognized Burke Burnet by his unusual size, and wondered what the boss man wanted. Just in case Burnet needed a fresh horse, Billy shook out a loop and flipped the noose over the neck of a long-muscled sorrel gelding that looked like it had plenty of bottom. The boss of an outfit wanted to be well mounted, thus Billy selected the best horse he could find.

Burnet trotted up and gave the sorrel a quick appraisal. "I see you've got an eye for horseflesh." He swung down and began to strip his saddle and bridle off a winded roan, talking while he went about making a saddle change. "Crawfish told me about a tangle you boys got in with Leon Pickett. Pickett's a no-good son of a bitch, and he's dangerous. Crawfish said you didn't act all that worried about him or his gun." Burnet cocked his head and looked Billy in the eye. "Are you any good with a pistol? Or was that just a bunch of wind?"

Billy wondered what sort of reply to give. "I never was in any kind of shoot-out with a hired gun, so I reckon it's hard for me to say, exactly. I ain't scared of him, if that's what you're askin'. He may be faster, but I'd call myself a decent shot at close range. The war taught me plenty of things, I suppose. I learned there's a time to run an' a time to fight if a man aims to stay alive. It ain't my nature to run from just one man, no matter if he's fast or just plain mean. But I don't want you to think I've got all that high an opinion of myself . . ."

Burnet continued to study him as he pulled his saddle off the roan. "I asked for a reason," he said, walking over to the sorrel with his rig. "I've got problems worse than getting this herd to Abilene. Back home, I've been losing cows to rustlers up in Indian Territory. The law won't go after them even when I try to raise a big stink, so I figure it's up to me to handle it my own way. Those cows and calves are carryin' my brand. It won't take a real smart feller to find 'em, but it may take a man with some backbone to fetch 'em back to my spread. I was wonderin' if that man might be you."

Billy thought about it after a shrug. "I wouldn't be any

opposed to lookin' for your cattle up yonder, if that's what you want. Kinda depends on how many rustlers took 'em, and how many cows I'd have to drive back if I found a way to get my hands on the bunch. If the trail is fresh, trackin' 'em oughta be easy.''

''I'd pay a sight better for some cattle detective work. A hundred a month, and expenses, to the right man.''

The amount made Billy whistle through his teeth. ''That's one hell of a pay raise, Mr. Burnet. I'd do a lot of lookin' for stolen cows at a hundred a month. Might' near guarantee I'd find them, too, if they ain't disappeared plumb off the face of the earth by now.''

''It's losing any more cows I'm worried about. They have got me figured for easy pickings, and I'll be away on this drive so I can't see to guarding the place myself. I'd pay you a hundred a month to poke around north of the Red River lookin' for the cows that got taken before, if I decide you're the man for the job. But my main worry is that they'll come back and cut another big slice off my mother cow herd while I'm gone up the Chisholm. I'd be gambling that you're good with a gun. You could bank on duckin' some lead if you ran across those rustlers . . . They won't give my cows up without a fight, if I'm any judge of bad character.''

''For that kind of money, I'd chance it.''

Burke studied him a moment more, then he mounted his sorrel and glanced toward the herd. ''I'll give the proposition a bit more thought. Asa recommended you highly, and vouched for your honesty. I need a good wrangler on this drive, but more than anything else I need someone who can find my stolen cattle and keep those owlhoots from rustling me again back home. We can talk about it after supper tonight.'' He touched a spur to the sorrel's ribs and struck a short lope back to the north.

''A hundred a month,'' Billy said aloud. ''I'd be rich by

the time Mr. Burnet got back from Kansas.'' The money set him to dreaming about ways to spend it. New boots, for sure, and some new duds, denims and shirts, a new beaver felt hat, maybe a good saddle, too. Right then he wasn't at all worried about dodging lead from outlaws' guns. He'd ducked Yankee rifle balls for four years and hardly got paid a cent.

With his mind full of sugar-plum thoughts, he crowded the remuda along in the cow herd's wake, hoping Burke would offer him the job. He could ask Asa about the ranch, what it was like, and everything he knew about the rustling going on. Burnet had said he'd be doing detective work. That had a nice ring to it, although later on he started to wonder if he could do the work—tracking rustlers down, using a gun when he had to.

Asa and Jimmie Dale rode back to change horses toward the middle of the afternoon. Billy couldn't wait to ask Asa about the ranch and tell him about the possibility of being a cattle detective. As soon as Asa swung down to strip his saddle, Billy began telling him about the job.

''A hundred dollars a month?'' Asa cried, like he had to ask to be sure he'd heard right. Then his expression changed. ''It would be real dangerous, Billy. Word is, it's Cherokee Bill's gang that hit us. Cherokee Bill Anderson is about the worst of all the badmen in Indian Territory. He's a half-breed, an outlaw who don't give a damn about the rewards posted for him no place else. He's safe in the Indian Nations, an' when he comes ridin' down on a ranch in Texas he comes well armed with three or four more of his kind. You could get your ass shot off. I'd think about that before I told the boss I'd take the money.''

''For a hundred a month I'll do might' near anything. I can worry about this Cherokee Bill when the time comes. If I could find Mr. Burnet's missing cattle, I just know I could figure a way to get 'em back.''

''It'll be real dangerous,'' Asa assured him. Then a slow smile tugged the corners of his mouth. ''There's a side benefit. The boss's daughter is mighty pretty to look at.''

''He didn't say nothin' about havin' a daughter back at the ranch . . .''

''Melissa's her name. Hair as black as a crow's feathers an' a face like a genuine angel. A bit on the uppity side, so she don't have much to do with ranch hands. But she's a beauty, like her ma, only younger.''

''There wouldn't be time to be lookin' at women if I was a cattle detective,'' Billy said. ''The boss made it sound like it was a full-time job.''

''Maybe,'' Asa remarked, sounding doubtful. ''There ain't any law close by, so you'd be on your own if there was trouble with Cherokee Bill. That's been the biggest problem, the fact that no law covers that part of the state. Texas Rangers don't hardly ever get out that way. Closest town with a lawman is Jacksboro, damn near a hundred miles . . .''

''One time, I gave some thought to the notion that I'd be a Texas Ranger. Until I found out that the pay is worse than bein' a cowboy.''

''Besides that, you'd be gettin' shot at most every day. A Ranger gets called to the most dangerous places all the time. I sure as hell wouldn't want no Rangerin' job.''

Billy hadn't been listening right then, thinking about the money Burnet was paying for detective work. At a hundred dollars a month, there was almost no risk he wouldn't be willing to take.

Asa saddled a black gelding and mounted. ''I'd think it over real good before I took that offer,'' he said. ''If it was Cherokee Bill an' his gang who hit us last month, you'd be in a worse fix than you was when Leon Pickett called you out this mornin', on account of you'll be on your own out at the ranch. There's old Juan, but he won't be much help if there was any shootin' to be done. He mostly fixes fence and looks after the women."

Once again, Billy wasn't listening. He'd already made up his mind. If the bossman offered him the detective job, he meant to take it. He'd done all the thinking he needed to do about a proposition paying him a hundred a month.

Asa and Jimmie Dale rode off, leaving Billy alone with his thoughts. This whole turn of events had started because he had found the courage to stand up to a gunfighter the other night.

"Sometimes it pays off to show a little backbone," he said to himself. Then he started to wonder if he'd simply been too drunk to realize what he was doing. This morning, facing Pickett again, his knees were trembling and he'd tasted fear on the tip of his tongue. Where had his backbone been then?

He wondered whether he had what it took to be a cattle detective facing a gang of badmen from the Nations. As the herd was being spread out to look for bed ground, Billy pushed the remuda toward the chuck wagon with his mind made up. If Burnet offered him the job, he would take it and let the chips fall in any manner they chose. William Jackson Blue was tired of being broke.

SEVEN

"Riders comin'!" someone shouted.

Against a sky pinked by sunset, five horsemen were outlined on a hilltop moving steadily toward the herd. Men gathered at the supper fire turned to watch the riders approach. A silence gripped the Burnet cowboys, for even from a distance everyone could see four of the men were carrying rifles.

"Been some kind of trouble," Burke said, tossing aside his tin plate of beans and stew meat. "They're all carryin' guns like they were after somebody . . ." He got up and looked at the faces around him. "Get your rifles from the back of the wagon, boys. I don't like the looks of this. It's too close to Fort Worth for them to be trail cutters, but all the same I want you to fetch those rifles."

Crawfish lifted the wagon sheet and began passing out .44-caliber Winchesters to Dutch, Little Luke, Sonny, and a rail-thin cowboy named Pete Jenkins. Asa took a rifle, but Billy decided against it for now, trying to see who the men were in poor light from a setting sun. He'd been eating stew and beans, thinking about his forthcoming talk with the boss regarding the detective job, and hadn't been the first to notice when men came riding off a ridge toward camp. They were still too far away to make them out clearly. Three night riders making wide circles around the herd watched the strangers head for the chuck wagon.

"They're comin' in," Burke said, working a cartridge into the firing chamber of his Winchester. "Wonder what the hell this is all about."

Suddenly, Billy knew what it was about. He dropped his food and got up slowly, watching a man in a flat brim approach aboard a big dappled gray horse. "The one in the middle is Leon Pickett," he said, taking the hammer thong from his heavy Colt. "I reckon it means they've come lookin' for me."

Burke aimed a stare at Billy, uncertain what to do. "This isn't our fight, Billy, but we won't let the five of them jump you like this. There's seven of us, not counting night riders. Surely Pickett is smart enough to know how to count."

Billy frowned, watching Pickett's easy way of sitting a horse. "I don't figure it has anything to do with you boys. He wants me to draw against him. His friends are along to make sure nobody else takes a hand in it. Pickett won't let it rest until he has satisfaction. Might as well decide it now . . ."

"That's plumb crazy, Billy!" Asa protested, shouldering the rifle in his hands. "It ain't a fair fight, you agin him."

"It's fair enough, I suppose. One man goin' up against the other, if that's the way he wants it. I figure he does."

"Sweet Jesus, Billy boy. Don't let him goad you into it."

"It don't appear he's gonna give me no other choice, Asa. I can't run off an' hide. He'll only keep lookin' for me."

"The dirty bastard," Burke hissed, scowling at the five as they came to the creek below the chuck wagon. "He knows he can win or he wouldn't be here. It'll be murder if I were to shoot him right here and now, but it crossed my mind."

Billy lifted his Walker a little higher in its holster to free it for a faster pull. Then he walked a slow circle around the fire and started down a grassy slope leading to the creek, which would take him to Pickett before he got to the chuck wagon.

"Please don't do this, Billy!" Asa pleaded. "We only got to get reacquainted today. We was gonna have us a barrel of fun up in Kansas . . ."

Billy ignored Asa's protest, striding toward the five men on horses trotting up the creek bank. He stopped on a level spot and waited there for Pickett and his companions to ride up, keeping his eyes on the rider in the middle flanked by men carrying rifles.

At thirty yards, Pickett signaled a halt. "You knew I was comin', didn't you? You knew I wasn't gonna let it end the way it did this mornin'."

"I figured as much. Climb down an' let's get this settled. My supper's gettin' cold." It was a brash thing to say and he wondered where the words had come from, like they spilled off the end of his tongue all by themselves.

The gunman handed one rein to a rider on his left and swung out of the saddle. "I brought some friends along, so none of those cowboys took a side in it this time." He tucked the tail of his black suit coat behind the butt of his pistol and squared himself in front of Billy. "You boys ride out of the way, just in case his aim ain't quite as good as he claims. He could get off a lucky shot even if I plug him dead-center."

The four riflemen reined out of harm's way, casting wary glances at the cowboys on the hill. "They got rifles, too, Leon," one of them said.

"They'll stay out of it," Billy promised. "I told them this was just between me an' him." Reflexively, his muscles tensed as he went into a half crouch, bending at the waist. His eyes were glued to Pickett's gun hand. He could feel his heart hammering inside his shirt, yet at the same time he felt that strange calm he'd noticed at the Pink Garter. It had nothing to do with whiskey after all, he told himself.

"Any time you're ready," Pickett growled, fingers curling on his right hand.

Billy waited, intent upon the other man's hand and gun. "I said I wouldn't draw on you first. The next move is yours . . ."

"You're a goddamn fool!" Pickett's hand dipped for his gun.

In the same instant Billy clawed for his Walker, his fingers closing around walnut grips, arm jerking the gun free of leather as fast as he could pull. Thumbing the hammer back while the gun came up in his fist. Aiming quickly. Pulling the trigger. A thundering explosion, the gun butt slamming into his palm as smoke curled away from the muzzle behind a finger of yellow flame.

Another explosion, muffled somewhat, and a flash of light from Pickett's revolver a split second later. Then a groan, a rush of air from a man's lungs, as Pickett was staggered by the passage of a lead slug through his breastbone, making a cracking noise like split kindling wood.

"Holy shit!" someone shouted from the hilltop behind Billy. "Did you see that? Billy shot first!"

Billy couldn't take his eyes off the gunman's lanky form as his feet shuffled backward from the force of a speeding bullet at close range. Pickett tried to get his footing, lost his balance, and toppled over on his back with a grunt. Then there was total silence, except for a horse snorting at the loud noises from the guns.

One of the four mounted men said, "I never woulda believed it if I hadn't seen it myself. You shot Leon before he got his gun clear—I seen him shoot a hole in the ground. Damned if I ever figured to see anybody drop him like that.'' The rifleman turned to look at Billy. ''He told us your name was Blue. Billy Blue was what he said your name was.''

Billy didn't answer, watching Pickett's right foot begin to twitch with death throes. Cowboys from the Burnet crew came down the hill slowly, spurs rattling over dry ground until they stood around Billy.

''He's dyin','' Billy said, when he noticed the presence of the others.

''Serves him right,'' Burke remarked, his voice a little on the thick side from watching a man take a bullet. ''He came here to kill you, only you were faster.''

''A hell of a lot faster,'' he heard Asa say. ''Sweet Jesus. I never figured you'd be quicker'n him, Billy boy.''

Everyone was watching Pickett. A wet, gurgling sound came from his throat, and from the war Billy knew that his slug had passed through a lung.

''He's liable to die slow,'' Crawfish offered. ''I can give the poor bastard a swallow of whiskey . . .''

''Maybe we oughta git him to a doctor,'' one of the riders said quietly, without much conviction.

''It's too late for that,'' another voice said, as a rifleman swung down to walk over to Pickett, peering down at him in the last rays of sunset from the west. ''He'll be dead in a couple of minutes. He's bleedin' like a hog at butcherin' time.''

Billy holstered his gun. Some part of him wanted to look into Leon Pickett's eyes before he died, while a gentler side of his nature said to walk away. But he listened to the inner voice that drew him to stand above the body, and when he gazed down upon the dying man's face, something inside him said he'd seen enough. Pickett's eyes were glazed over, staring up blankly at the evening sky. ''You should have left it alone'' was all Billy could think of to whisper, before he turned away and began walking slowly back up the hill to their camp fire on legs that felt like they were made of cast iron.

Asa caught up to him. ''You okay, Billy?''

He could barely manage a nod. ''I reckon I could use a drink of whiskey,'' he said later, when his breath returned. ''I've got a jug in my saddlebags.'' He leaned against a wheel of the chuck wagon when he noticed his head was swimming. The cold realization struck him now that he had killed a man in a duel. It was not anything like the killing he'd done during the war . . . That had had a sense of duty attached to it. Shooting Pickett left him with an empty feeling. And his hands were shaking.

''Damn but you was fast,'' Asa said, interrupting his thoughts abruptly. ''Where'd you learn to draw an' shoot like that?''

''Fetch that whiskey, pardner'' was all he said, staring off at the first stars of night in a darkening sky.

Asa wheeled away to look for the bottle. It was then Billy saw the other cowboys watching him from the far side of the fire pit. They were staring at him, looking at him differently in a way he couldn't explain.

''Hope I didn't ruin your supper,'' he told them, remembering his plate of stew, not hungry for it now.

Burke trudged up the hill. Behind him, the men who'd come with Pickett were hoisting his body over the back of his gray horse. Burke walked to the fire. ''He's dead,'' the rancher said solemnly, looking straight at Billy.

''He drew on me first, Mr. Burnet.''

''We all saw it. He provoked you into a fight. You're real fast with a gun, Billy. Fastest man I ever saw.''

Perhaps it was meant as a compliment, but when Billy heard it he looked askance like he was embarrassed. Asa hurried over with the whiskey and uncorked it. Scenting sweet barley vapors coming from the neck, Billy took a deep swallow and let out a sigh. "Thanks, hoss," he said hoarsely, feeling a burn all the way down his throat.

The sounds of moving horses reached the chuck wagon. A man leading the dappled gray with Pickett's body lashed to the saddle rode ahead of the others back to the east. Billy watched their grim procession move away into the darkness, wondering if he had changed somehow. He felt different inside, neither good nor bad in any particular way. Different.

"Word's gonna spread all over Hell's Half Acre," Asa remarked as the horsemen rode out of sight. "Everybody is gonna know who done this to Leon Pickett. They'll be talkin' about this shootin' in every saloon in Satan's backyard. You'll be famous before sunrise as the feller who outgunned Leon."

While it was probably true that he would have a reputation now as a shootist, it was something Billy didn't care to hear just then. "Let it rest for a minute, pardner. I ain't exactly in a talkin' mood right now," he said quietly.

Boots clumped toward him from the direction of the fire as Burke came over. "You proved you can handle yourself with a gun to my satisfaction," the rancher said, resting his hands on his hips while trying to read Billy's face in the half dark. "If you want that job lookin' for my stolen cattle and keeping an eye on the ranch while we're on the trail, it's yours. In the morning I can give you directions, and a letter to my wife and daughter so they'll know I sent you. If you need it, you can have more time to think it over . . ."

Billy wagged his head. "Fix up that letter, Mr. Burnet. I'll start out for the ranch at first light. I'll do the best I can to find your stolen beef an' keep an eye on things."

Burke extended his hand. They shook on it. And with that handshake Billy understood how it was he had changed. He wasn't simply a cowboy any longer . . . A hired gun was what he had become.

EIGHT

He led his spare horse across dry rangeland, a good liver chestnut gelding from the remuda that would enable him to ride Burnet Ranch pastures on a fresh mount. He was aimed for Red River country northwest of Fort Worth, beyond a settlement named Wichita Falls, which he was told was little more than a buffalo hunters' camp. Buffalo hunters had begun to comb the western frontier killing animals solely for their hides, leaving rotting carcasses everywhere they went, a further irritant to the Plains Indians who depended on buffalo for meat and skins to make it through the winter. Comanches were the most troublesome, and the most warlike, in the region south of the Red, Burnet said. But Indians from all over the Territory north of the river had begun raiding Texas ranches, and along with them came half-breed opportunists like Cherokee Bill and more of his kind, who plundered cow herds and homesteads simply for the profit in it.

With a letter of introduction in his saddlebags, Billy made for the ranch wondering how difficult his job would be—trying to keep rustlers from striking the Burnet herds again. And in the back of his mind he tried to visualize what it would be like when he set out to track Burnet's missing cows into the Nations. It was a lawless place, ruled by Kiowa and Osage and Comanche bands on the prowl for booty. A handful of federal marshals attempted to police the most populated areas and keep watch over the cattle trails to prevent wholesale outlawry against herds moving up to the Kansas railheads. But for the most part the effort was in vain, and the wisest trail foremen simply paid tolls in the form of lame cattle to starving Indian tribes whose land they crossed along the Chisholm.

Billy knew it would be no easy task, tracking Burnet's cows. By now most or all of the cattle sign would be lost to the passage of time. According to Burke, the rustlers hit his herd for the second time a little more than three weeks back, leaving a trail anyone could follow to the Red River, where tracks crossed over into Indian Territory. And twice Burnet wired the U.S. Marshal's office for the Territory at Fort Smith to request an investigation, only to be informed by a terse telegram that overworked marshals could only look into the rustling later in the summer.

"Wish Asa could have ridden along," Billy said. Protecting a far-flung cow-and-calf operation, spread out over forty sections of land, was hardly a one-man job. And if he went across the Red looking for Burke's missing beeves, it would leave the ranch easy prey to another raid by Cherokee Bill's gang. Juan, the old vaquero who was the only man about the place, was too stove-up in his joints from a fall off a bucking horse to do much riding. Juan was charged with keeping watch over the women at the ranch—Burnet's wife and daughter. Burke was gambling by leaving his ranch unprotected while he drove his beef to the railheads, although cowmen had no choice but to get their calves to market. And now Billy had responsibility for the cow herd.

"It pays a hundred a month," he told himself again.

Later that afternoon he began to encounter buffalo bones on the prairies. Skeletons lay everywhere he looked, picked clean by buzzards and coyotes until bones lay among scattered clumps of gamma grass in every direction, bleached by the relentless West Texas sun to a pale white hue. Bones looked out of place amid lush green grasslands where spring had begun to renew last year's growth. They served as a reminder to every Indian that white men meant to destroy the Indians' way of life. "It's damn little wonder those redskins hate us," he mumbled. Talking to himself was a habit developed on long rides alone, and he thought nothing of the fact that no one was there to hear him. Most cowboys he knew admitted to carrying on long conversations with themselves during solitary moments. A cowboy's existence was usually lonely, since much of the work only required one man. Until fall roundups or spring cattle drives came, most ranch work was performed by a single cowhand. Men who needed a lot of company seldom made cowboying a profession.

Crossing a string of rocky hills studded with scrub mesquite trees, he saw more empty miles in front of him. With nothing to occupy his mind, he allowed himself to remember the gunfight with Pickett. All morning he'd tried to shut it out of his thoughts as best he could. Killing a man in a duel, even a man who by all accounts needed killing, gave him an uncomfortable feeling in the pit of his stomach. He had crossed an imaginary line last night, a line drawn by his conscience. Always before, there had been a reason for the killing he'd done—a war, a cause he believed in and orders from someone in command. But with yesterday's gunfight all that had changed. And he had changed along with it.

He wondered if he were truly faster with a gun. Or had it simply been luck? He recalled how he felt just before the fight commenced—the calm, a feeling that things would turn out the way he hoped they would. How had he known he was quicker? What was it that convinced him he could survive Pickett's deadly gun? Or had he only been trying to fool himself . . .

He remembered Pickett's sightless eyes moments before death claimed him, and he shuddered. There was no feeling of victory, winning a contest at the draw against him. It was as if there was no emotion attached to it whatsoever.

As dusk approached Billy scanned the prairie for a campsite offering water for his horses. And a soft spot where he hoped to be able to sleep. He'd hardly slept at all the night before, gazing up at the stars, remembering his duel. Tonight, with the help of some of the whiskey in his saddlebags, he meant to remedy that if he could.

He found a stream just as dusk became dark, with grazing for his horses. Underneath a skyful of twinkling stars he built a fire and hobbled his animals before setting out to fix himself a supper of cold biscuits and hot coffee laced heavily with whiskey.

They were a pitiful-looking lot, five hungry Indians leading two starving ponies northward from the mouth of a draw just after the sun came up. Shrouded in worn blankets against a lingering chill after a cold night on the high plains in March, they walked out of the draw and appeared to be surprised to find him riding toward them. The Indian at the front of the procession, a man in ragged buckskin leggings carrying an old musket and powder horn, made a show of putting down his weapon. A slender woman walking behind him wheeled around and gestured to her three children to lie down in the grass.

Billy had been just as surprised to find anyone else in the empty, broken country around him. Until now he'd only seen deer and a few antelope, an occasional jackrabbit. Finding Indians, even a starving bunch like this, awakened him from a daze to the dangers that could be lurking just out of sight over the next ridge or hiding in the maze of winding dry washes crisscrossing this region. Armed with a Winchester rifle Burnet had given him from the chuck wagon armory, he could defend himself. But when he got a closer look at the Indians, he was certain he wouldn't be needing his guns. The Indian family was a tragic sight and their ponies were nothing but skin and bones.

He rode toward them at a jog trot, making up his mind that he would offer them some of the dry beans and salt pork he had in his saddlebags—Crawfish had given him more than he would need. As he trotted closer to the Indians, he noticed bulky packs wrapped in animal skins on the backs of their ponies, most likely everything they owned and a buffalo-hide tent. The man stood showing his empty hands while the woman knelt with her children near the horses. When Billy got closer, he could see the fear on their faces.

He slowed his horse to a walk and drew rein a few yards from them before he reached into his saddlebags. The skinny warrior watched him impassively, still showing that his hands were empty. When Billy took out a sack of dry pintos, the Indian's eyes were on the bag.

"Here's some food. I can see you an' your kids are hungry. Wish I had more to share with you." He tossed the bag down, and when it struck the ground, the binding string broke, spilling beans over the gamma grass. The Indian made no move to come for the sack, watching Billy's face.

"Here's a little salted meat to go with 'em," Billy added, taking out a bundle of bacon wrapped in oilcloth. With an old Barlow pocketknife he cut off a chunk and held it out for the Indian to see. "Come get it. It ain't much, but it's all I can spare . . ."

A moment passed before the Indian understood. He took a few uncertain steps forward, hesitating, until he could reach for the bacon on the end of the knife blade. He said, "*Samon po-mero,*" in a quiet, guttural voice, fingering the greasy salt pork while he backed away from Billy's horse to pick up the sack of beans.

Then the Indian did a downright unusual thing—he took a string of beads and animal claws from around his neck, passing it over his twin braids of coal black hair. He came forward again and offered it up to Billy.

"I don't want your necklace," Billy explained, shaking his head side to side. "The food's a gift for those hungry kids an' your wife. I felt sorry for you, on account of I know what it's like to be real hungry."

It was evident the Indian did not understand, for he stood with the necklace in an outstretched hand, waiting for Billy to take it from him.

"I don't reckon you speak no English."

"*Samon po-mero,*" the skinny warrior said again.

And so Billy took the beads and claws, not wanting to make an issue of the trade the Indian was offering. He grinned and closed his pocketknife, put the rest of the bacon away, and hung the necklace around his neck. "Thanks," he said, not knowing what else to say or do. He raised a palm and waved good-bye, and as he reined his horse away, he glanced at the woman and her children. They remained huddled in front of the stunted ponies to watch him ride off.

"At least their kids will have somethin' to eat," he said, urging both horses to a lope.

Once, before he rode out of sight, he took a look over his shoulder. The Indians were gathered around the spilled beans, picking them up a few at a time.

As the horses crested a hill, Billy lifted the string of beads and claws, examining it more closely. The beads were of little value, probably trade goods, but the claws and talons and teeth at the end of the rawhide loop held his attention for a time. He was sure the necklace had great value to the man who gave it to him, and for this reason alone he decided to wear it, at least for now. Feeding five hungry Indians made him feel a little better this morning, after a night of tossing and turning in his bedroll, remembering the gunfight.

Galloping past more buffalo bones, he felt a touch of sorrow for what was happening to the Indians' homeland. White men were bent on changing the face of the earth along the western frontier, and nothing would stop them from building settlements and plowing up the prairies. Gazing across open expanses lying before him, Billy knew he was seeing the beginning of an end to this unsettled land. Before long fences would cut these plains into squares, and that would be the last of it for free-roaming men of every color. Sad, he thought, that most people couldn't leave things the way they found them.

All day, as he pushed his horses across empty miles of sage and mesquite prairie, he encountered no one, nor was there any sign of civilization beyond a few faint traces of wagon roads in a place or two. Off to the west flat-topped mesas cast purple shadows late in the afternoon, with the sun dropping low in the skies behind them. Puffy clouds drifted southward on gusts of warm wind, providing a beautiful vista when darkness crept over the land, clouds with their underbellies reddened by a brilliant crimson sunset.

His horses scattered quail and prairie hens away from a bend in a creek lined with cottonwoods after he crested a hill above the stream. He could hear the wind rustling cottonwood leaves in a moment of silence as he rode down to the water. Upstream, a deer bounded away from a stand of brush, then two more, a doe and a buck following the first deer away from the creek. Billy watched their graceful strides for a moment while his horses drank their fill from the shallows. He felt total contentment right then, with so much raw beauty around him. At times like these he knew why he was drawn to a cowboy's life. There was a peace out here in open country and a solitude that somehow nurtured him, giving strength to an inner part of him when nothing else could.

"I'd sure as hell hate to give this up," he said quietly, as he looked around him.

When the horses were watered, he swung down to look for firewood and rocks to form a fire pit below a cut bank above the creek that would be out of sight from the prairies, should any travelers happen along during the night. Other than happening upon the starving Indians this morning, he hadn't seen another soul since he left the herd.

"Suits me, bein' all by my lonesome," he muttered, stripping off his saddle and applying hobbles to both horses where new spring grass grew thick beside the stream.

He took out a pint of whiskey and drained the bottle, sighing when he contemplated the empty container. "I sure hope I can sleep," he said, knowing that he probably couldn't. He tossed the bottle aside and found a place to spread his bedroll before he built a fire.

NINE

A horse snorted somewhere in the darkness. Billy raised his head, blinking sleep fog from his eyes, trying to clear his brain and get his bearings. One of the horses sensed something in the night, a presence close by that was unfamiliar. Was it a coyote or a wolf? Or a more formidable danger?

Coals glowed faintly in the fire pit, giving off only a meager circle of light. He reached for the Winchester lying beside him and drew it slowly across his chest before working the mechanism quietly, levering a shell into the chamber. As carefully as he could, he rolled out of his blankets and came to a crouch, scanning the dark, searching for the outlines of his horses against an inky sky dotted with pale stars. Farther downstream, he found a shape moving into the trees. Someone was leading one of Billy's horses away from the creek, and the instant he saw it, he swung the rifle to his shoulder, resting his sights on the silhouette of a man.

He squeezed the Winchester's trigger gently. A roar shattered the night silence, echoing through cottonwood trunks like a mighty peal of thunder from stormy skies. A thin shaft of yellow light accompanied the explosion, slicing through black shadows toward a line of trees. The gun slammed into Billy's right shoulder, rocking him backward, and although his ears rang from the rifle blast, he could hear a cry near the water's edge plainly enough. The silhouette fell limply to the ground while his horse bolted away, snorting when it splashed into the creek at a gallop.

Billy ejected the spent cartridge as he was running to a tree trunk for protection, in the event more than one horse thief was hidden in the cottonwood forest. Panting, suddenly wide awake now, he searched the shadows for movement while listening to the thump of running hooves moving farther downstream. The would-be thief had taken his hobbles off the horse, and now it was running free—he had to catch it soon or the animal would be lost before morning. He could make out another horse lunging up the creek bank with its forelegs still in hobbles, thus he had a horse to ride if the shot ended further attempts to rustle his livestock. Darting from one cottonwood trunk to the next with his rifle ready, he moved as quickly as he dared toward the hobbled horse without making a target of himself.

He reached the chestnut gelding and tried to calm it with his voice, saying, "Whoa there, boy. Easy now." Sweeping the trees and surrounding brush with a careful look, he saw no one else in the dark and walked cautiously to his horse and began stroking its neck gently. Then he heard a muffled groan coming from the far side of the creek. The man he shot had been mortally wounded, judging by his quiet cries.

Billy walked down to the water and waded across with his gun covering the opposite bank, sweeping the muzzle back and forth until he saw a dark shape lying in a patch of grass below shadows cast from cottonwood limbs. Another moan came from the spot as he was creeping toward the body, wondering if his victim might be concealing a pistol beneath him, waiting for a chance to even the score. The noise from wet boots announced his stealthy approach no matter how quietly he tried to move on the balls of his feet to the base of a tree.

"Oh no," he whispered, when he saw a woman lying near him. She wore a stained buckskin dress with ragged fringe, and even in bad light he recognized her. His nostrils filled with the scent of blood as he knelt beside the Indian woman he had encountered coming out of the draw earlier this morning.

Remembering the skinny warrior, he cast another wary look around him. Why had the woman come to steal his horses? Where was the warrior who was with her? Billy remembered an ancient musket the Indian carried . . . was it aimed at him now from some hiding place in the forest?

Yet no matter how carefully he examined his surroundings, he found nothing amiss, no sign of the Indian who had accompanied the woman and children when he gave them some of his provisions. It made little sense that the woman had been the one to slip up to his camp alone and steal his animals.

He gazed down at her again, examining her ragged dress and her twin braids of black hair spread on the grass where she had fallen facedown. A dark hole near her left shoulder glistened wetly in weak starlight—the blood smell grew stronger. The bullet hole was high, missing vital organs.

"Hey, lady," he whispered hoarsely, still wary of announcing his position with the sound of his voice. "Do you understand any English?"

A moan answered him. He could see that her hands were empty, and thus he felt safe when he put his rifle aside before he touched her gently.

The woman's eyes opened. Very slowly, she turned her face to him, blinking. When she saw him, she tried to shrink away in the grass.

"I won't hurt you again, lady. Do you understand me? You was tryin' to steal my horses, so I had to stop you."

Her eyes were fixed on his, but she said nothing and he was sure she spoke no English. Still troubled by the absence of the Indian warrior, he studied the trees again.

"Can't figure why you came alone," he said, more to himself than the woman since she couldn't understand him. He didn't hear hoofbeats any longer. His bay was somewhere out on the prairie. Startled by the gunshot, it could run for miles before it stopped to graze. At sunrise he should be able to track it down, unless it fell into the hands of the warrior during the night.

He examined her wound as closely as he could in the darkness and said, "I can put a bandage around it. Maybe splash a little whiskey in it to keep it from festerin' too bad. No tellin' how far it is to the closest doctor, lady. I'm downright sorry I put a bullet through you, but after all, you was tryin' to steal my horses an' I couldn't just let you take 'em."

Again he got no response from her, no sign of recognition in her face when he spoke. He pondered his dilemma briefly. He had a responsibility to the injured woman even though she had been trying to steal his animals. He couldn't simply leave her to die slowly from a wound. According to the directions Burke Burnet gave him, he was only a day's ride, more or less, from the ranch.

"Maybe there'll be somebody at the Burnet spread who knows how to take care of you. I can't just leave you layin' here or you'll bleed to death." Having said this, he wondered how to carry her to the ranch. "I'll have to find my bay so you'll be able to ride. I reckon I can hold you in the saddle in front of me if you can't sit by your lonesome. I sure do wish you could talk to me, lady. At least understand what I'm sayin' to you."

When it was clear the woman was too weak to rise on her own even if he gave her assistance, he put both arms underneath her and lifted her gently off the ground. She whimpered softly when movement caused her pain, yet she offered no resistance as he took her down to the stream, leaving his rifle and horse behind for the moment. His chestnut had settled and returned to grazing in tall grass above the creek—he knew he was taking a risk leaving his horse and gun unattended for even a moment. Hurrying toward the red glow of his fire's embers, he glanced over his shoulder from time to time until he reached his bedroll, where he put the woman down gently atop his blankets.

He strapped on his Colt. "I'll be right back, lady," he said quietly, watching the trees around them, still wondering why the woman's husband had not shown up after the gunshot. Was it some sort of Indian custom to send women off to steal horses by themselves? He strode away from the fire carrying a rope halter, recalling how thin and forlorn those Indian children looked this morning, hoping they'd had a chance to eat the beans and bacon he gave them.

After retrieving his horse and rifle, he came back to the fire to saddle the chestnut gelding, deciding he needed to make an attempt to find his bay before sunrise. But the first order of business was to clean and dress the bullet hole in the woman's shoulder. It was a shame to waste good whiskey, what little he had left, cleaning a wound rather than for drinking. But after he thought on it some, it seemed the very least he could do, seeing as it was his bullet that caused the damage.

He took out his whiskey and knelt beside her when fingers of flame darted from a handful of dry wood he put on the coals. He found the woman staring at him when light showed him her face, and as his gaze moved down to her wound, he couldn't help but wince a little. Blood streamed down her dress from a ragged tear in the buckskin below her shoulder. "At least the bullet came out," he muttered under his breath.

He took his bandanna and soaked it with whiskey, and

as he leaned down to dab the cloth against her shoulder, the woman drew back, wrinkling her nose.

"I know it kinda smells bad," he said, grinning. "To tell the truth it don't taste all that good either, but sometimes it sure helps a feller fall off to sleep when he can't otherwise."

As soon as the bandanna touched her torn flesh, the woman let out a gasp, pulling away from him, crawling backward on the pile of blankets. "Take it easy, lady," he told her gently, even with the knowledge that she couldn't understand him, hoping that the tone of his voice would calm her some. He would have to tear his spare shirt into strips in order to fashion a bandage that would fit around her. Now and then he glanced at the trees for sign of the warrior as he went about making a wound dressing out of his only extra shirt. Several times he looked more closely at the woman's face, finding that she was almost pretty.

Later, after her bleeding stopped, he had to sear the bullet hole with the heated tip of his knife to keep the wound from festering. He hoped he could make her understand that it was necessary to keep her alive, a helluva job, since she didn't appear to understand a single word he said.

TEN

Billy's nose wrinkled and he came partially awake to the delicious smell of Arbuckle's boiling over an open fire. He rolled over, squinting against a dawn sunrise, enjoying brilliant hues of orange and red playing on the underside of morning clouds on the horizon.

A hissing, crackling sound brought him fully awake with a start, thinking at first a rattler had crawled into camp. He bolted upright, his hand reflexively clawing for his Walker, trying to shake sleep fog from his mind.

The Indian woman was bent over the fire, clutching her left arm tight against her side as she stirred something in a cast iron skillet propped on three rocks at the edge of a bed of glowing coals.

What the hell? he thought, scrambling to his feet before hurrying over to the fire. "You shouldn't oughta be doin' that, ma'am," he said, grabbing the handle of the pan away from her. "You're liable to get that wound to bleedin' again."

She shrunk back from him, eyes wide as if staring at a madman. He lowered his voice a mite, trying to sound less angry or threatening. "It's not that I don't 'preciate it an' all, I just don't want you to hurt yourself on my account.''

He glanced down at the skillet and saw a mess of scrambled eggs bubbling next to thick slices of bacon fatback, the aroma making his mouth water and his stomach growl.

Where in the hell did she get eggs? he wondered, shaking his head. Then he spied six quail eggshells broken on the ground next to her. She must have gotten up before dawn and searched the brush for those eggs, and her with that bad arm that must be hurting something fierce, he figured. ''If I live to be a hundred,'' he muttered as he stirred the eggs and bacon so they wouldn't burn, ''I'll never understand females. Here you come into my camp to try an' help me by catching my horse 'fore it runs away, an' I repay you by shootin' a hole in you, an' next mornin' you get up an' fix me breakfast.''

The woman arched an eyebrow, almost as if she could understand what he was saying, though she had yet to speak a single word in his company.

Billy scraped the food into two tin plates and handed one to her. She took it tentatively, as if she wasn't used to a man sharing his food with her. He wrapped his bandanna around the handle of the coffeepot and filled two tin cups with the steaming black brew, then sat cross-legged and began to eat. It was the most delicious meal, he believed, he'd ever eaten.

Neither spoke or made any sounds until the eggs and bacon and coffee were gone . . . The woman ate with her fingers, as though a tin spoon was an unfamiliar thing. After Billy took his last bite, scraping his plate clean, she got to her feet, took his plate and cup and the skillet, and walked slowly toward the creek, bent over a little like her arm was still hurting.

While she was scrubbing the utensils with wet sand to clean them, he broke camp, saddling his chestnut and putting a rope halter on the bay. He threw his spare blanket over the bay's back and smothered out the fire as she packed the plates and cups in his saddlebags.

"Do you think you can ride by yourself, or should I put you on the chestnut with me?" he asked, not really expecting an answer, merely talking to be making one-sided conversation like he always did on the trail . . . A while back he'd concluded that he must have worn out the ears on several good horses.

She didn't answer him, yet she grabbed the bay's mane with her right hand and swung up on its back effortlessly, her face drawn tight from pain in her wounded shoulder.

"I reckon that answers my question," he said. He stepped into the saddle and reined his horse toward the western horizon, hoping to find the Burnet ranch early today, to keep the girl from suffering any longer than necessary from the jolting gait of the horse.

As they rode through rolling hills thick with mesquite and live oak trees, spring wildflowers splashing brilliant colors of blue, red, and yellow everywhere, Billy continued to talk, not really saying anything of importance, just making noise to make time pass.

"I killed this owlhoot by the name of Leon Pickett, an' I sure do hope I won that gunfight because I was better with a gun, not because some famous gunhawk was drunk, or hung over, or sick or somethin'. I've allowed as how I ain't all that sure I don't have a touch of yellow streak in me, since I still get a mite weak-kneed at the thought of facing down a shooter with Pickett's reputation. Even though somethin' good came out of it, I still don't much cotton to the notion that I killed a man for no good reason. If he'd've just let it alone, I'd still be wranglin' an' he'd still be breathin' air, 'stead of deader'n that fatback we ate this mornin'."

He looked back at the woman to see if she was listening to him. He couldn't tell, for her eyes were fixed straight ahead, slitted a little against the pain the jostling of the horse must be causing in her arm. At least she had a bit more color in her face this morning; brown as an acorn, instead of pasty white like she was last night.

Billy studied the horizon, thinking it must be true what white men said about Indians, how they don't feel pain like normal folks. He'd seen lots of boys in the war get the hot iron treatment, and nary a one of them had failed to scream like they was being killed. She'd only grunted and moaned a little as the iron fried her flesh. He shuddered at the remembrance, knowing he'd not have been so brave had it been him under the knife.

"I reckon when we get to the Burnet ranch, I'll be sendin' you on your way. I got me a job as a detective, so I'm gonna hunt down Mr. Burnet's missing beeves an' see if'n I've got the nerve to try an' take 'em back from that Cherokee Bill an' his friends."

He was silent for a few miles, thinking on how he would go about tracking down the steers and what he'd need to take with him on the trip. Plenty of .44 shells, that was for sure. It's a good thing the Winchester and my Walker both use the same ammunition, he thought. Be less to carry on the trail. Still, I'm gonna need a pack horse, and maybe a Sharps long-shooter rifle if they've got one at the ranch. Be a lot safer to fire down on those boys from a long ways off, if I can.

As they rode, Billy talking while the Indian stared straight ahead, silent, the miles melted away. A spring sun warmed the air to a comfortable temperature, far below the furnace heat that would come with summer in this region. Since he was getting low on rations, Billy elected not to stop for a nooning to make camp. He did rein to a halt, passing the woman a couple of cold biscuits and a cut of jerked meat to eat, now and then handing his canteen back and forth to wash the dry food down before continuing on their way.

About an hour before dusk they came over a ridge and saw a ranch house with a barn and corrals in a shallow valley below. A few hundred longhorn cows and bulls were grazing near the pens, but he could see no cowboys, or anyone else for that matter, in the vicinity of the ranch.

"I figure that's where we're headed," he said over his shoulder. He heeled his chestnut off the ridge with the girl clinging to the bay's back, slumped over the horse's withers as proof the ride had been hard on her, painful.

When he was a hundred yards from the main house, a short, bowlegged man in a large sombrero stepped onto the front porch, a Greener scattergun cradled in his arms, a scowl on his face not hidden by his hat brim or a drooping handlebar mustache.

He held up a hand, signaling Billy to halt right where he was. "*Ola*, señor," the man said in a thick Mexican accent.

Having grown up in Texas, riding with plenty of vaqueros on cow trails, Billy knew a little Tex-Mex, enough to get by most times. "*Ola, señor*," he answered, keeping his hands out in plain sight, the Greener making him cautious. He didn't care to get blasted to eternity before he had a chance to identify himself.

"My name's Billy Blue, Señor, an' Mr. Burnet sent me. I got his letter here in my saddlebags. Can we climb down?"

The old vaquero tilted his head as he considered what Billy said. He spoke over his shoulder in a low voice Billy couldn't make out, to someone behind the doorway. After a bit, listening to a muffled reply, he stepped off the porch and walked a few paces from the house, still holding the express gun at the ready.

"Come down, señor, and let me see this letter."

Billy and the Indian walked their horses forward until

they were a bit closer, then he dismounted, still keeping his hand away from his gun. He pulled the letter out and handed it to the Mexican, who opened the paper carefully, holding it close to his face while his eyes narrowed as if he were nearsighted.

That's why he's using a scattergun, Billy thought, because he can't see well enough to use a pistol.

After reading the contents of the letter twice, the old man turned toward the house and said, "Miss Burnet, you better come out here."

A young woman, who appeared to be in her twenties, stepped through the doorway onto the porch. She held a Henry repeating rifle in her hands as if she knew how to use it. She stood there for a moment, staring first at Billy, then at the Indian woman still seated on the horse behind him.

As she walked down the steps toward them, Billy's heart fluttered in his chest. He thought she was the most beautiful girl he had ever seen—just over five feet tall, with dark eyes, a dusting of freckles across her cheeks, and coal black hair hanging down to the middle of her back. She wore denim jeans and a man's shirt with the sleeves rolled up, both tight enough to show plenty of curves in all the right places, and carried a small pistol, probably a .32-caliber, in a holster on her right hip.

She took the letter from the vaquero and read it, frowning. "Well, what do you think, Juan? This letter says Dad was sending a man named Billy Blue, but it doesn't mention him bringing his squaw with him."

At the word "squaw," Billy noticed the Indian's eyes narrow, just for a moment, then her faraway stare and impassive face returned.

"Excuse me, ma'am, but she ain't exactly my squaw. I met her on the way here an' gave her family some of my food since they looked like they was starvin'. Later on, by mistake, I shot her in the shoulder an' almost killed her. I patched her up best I could and brought her here to get taken care of till she's well enough to ride on."

The girl's pretty face turned ugly as she sneered, "That was right neighborly of you, Mr. Blue." She handed the letter back to Juan and walked away, saying, "Find out what's going on, Juan, and set Mr. Blue and his . . . friend up in the bunkhouse. I'll talk to Mom and see what she wants to do about all this."

Billy touched his hat, replying softly, with more than a pinch of sarcasm of his own, "Nice to meet you, too, Miz Burnet."

The girl hesitated, breaking stride briefly, then squared her shoulders and continued on her way to the house.

Juan grinned, a gold tooth sparking in the late afternoon sunlight. "Come with me, Señor Blue, an' we will get you set up."

As the Indian woman dismounted, Juan tipped his sombrero and said, "*Como esta, señorita?*"

She lowered her eyes and replied, "*Bien.*"

Billy slapped his thigh. "Well, I'll be damned! Juan, find out what her name is."

Juan asked the question in Spanish and she answered in a soft, almost shy voice, "Pia."

Billy asked, "What's that mean in Mexican, Juan?"

Juan glanced at Billy, an eyebrow raised. "That means nothing in *Espanol,* señor, however, it means 'arrow' in the Comanche tongue."

"Oh . . . arrow, huh?" Billy said. "I don't know no Comanch', but I do know a little Mex, I just never figured to use it on her."

Juan spoke to the woman for another few minutes as he led them to the bunkhouse. "She is of the Comanche tribe, Señor Billy. She says her husband traded her to you for food for their children, and that now she is your property."

"Now, hold on there, Juan. I never agreed to no trade. I just gave them some beans an' fatback."

Juan pointed to the necklace around Billy's neck. "When you took that, it means you accepted the trade, señor. I'm afraid she is yours now."

Billy stopped walking and put his hand on Pia's shoulder, causing her to wince with pain. "Just a minute, Juan. You tell Pia for me that the trade is off. I ain't gonna take no Indian woman to raise, 'specially not for no reason on earth."

After speaking to the girl again in Spanish, Juan looked at Billy, grinning. "I told her, señor. However, like all women, she is stubborn. She says she belongs to you and that is the end of it."

"Damn," Billy whispered, then he stomped off toward the bunkhouse, muttering, "As if I don't have enough troubles with rustlers an' bandidos an' such. I don't need no other distractions till this stolen cattle business is taken care of."

ELEVEN

Billy marched toward the bunkhouse, kicking up dust clouds with his boots, talking to himself, "I swear women were put on this earth purely to be an aggravation for men. Hell, if there weren't no women around, couldn't hardly get no one to be a cowboy . . . There'd be no reason to head out on a lonesome trail for months on end."

After a few steps, he heard a grunt behind him, and Juan whispered, "*Madre de Dios!* Señor Blue . . ."

Billy looked back and saw Pia slumped in Juan's arms, head hanging limp, face a pasty white, unconscious. "Damn, now what?" he said as he rushed to help support her. "What happened, Juan?"

"I do not know, señor. She was following you and her eyes got funny and rolled back and she staggered. I grab her just before she fall."

Billy laid the back of his hand on the young woman's sweat-covered face. "Jesus, she's burning up with fever. Let's get her to the bunkhouse, pronto."

After carrying Pia into the cabin, Billy and Juan stretched her out on one of the bunks. Billy took his bandanna, dipped it in a bucket of drinking water, and began to swab her face and neck. "Juan, you'd better go get Mrs. Burnet and see if she has any medicine or poultices an' such that might help Pia. It appears she's not doin' as well as she pretended."

"*Sí,* señor, I go very fast."

While he waited for Juan to return, Billy continued to sponge her face, speaking to her in a low voice, hoping she couldn't tell how worried he was. "I guess I just thought I was done with you causing me trouble, Pia. Course, I can't blame you overly much, since it was my bullet caused it."

He peeled back a shoulder of her dress to look at her wound. It was puffy, surrounded by inflamed tissues. There was no pus yet, for which he was thankful, knowing pus would mean death could not be avoided.

After a few minutes, a striking woman walked into the bunkhouse, her long strides having left Juan hobbling on arthritic knees far behind. Billy looked up, pleased by what he saw. Mrs. Burnet looked like a rancher's wife—dressed in denims and low-cut boots with a flannel man's shirt on, sleeves rolled up to show dirt-smudged arms and hands. Billy thought, This is a woman who does her share of the work, not like that spoiled-rotten daughter of hers.

Mrs. Burnet was attractive, in a rugged sort of way. Her hair was cut short, practical, and her face was bronze with plenty of sun wrinkles, but they were mostly around the eyes, making Billy think this was someone who laughed a lot. He liked her right off, before she said a word, knowing somehow this was a lady who would stand by her man against Indians, bad weather, and anything else that might have come their way while they were carving a ranch out of this wilderness.

He nodded and said, "Howdy, ma'am," continuing to swipe his damp bandanna across Pia's face.

Mrs. Burnet stood over the bunk a moment, looking

down at him with her hands on her hips. "Good afternoon, Mr. Blue. My name is Mary Elizabeth Burnet." One side of her mouth curled up in what might have been a smile, but Billy couldn't be sure. "I hear you've already met my daughter."

"Yes, ma'am, and Juan, too."

"Good. We'll talk more later about why my husband sent you, but now tell me about this young woman. My daughter told me she was wounded but that she didn't think it was too bad."

"I put a bullet though her left shoulder yesterday evenin', thinkin' she was rustlin' my horses. She wasn't, it turned out, so I tried all I knew to take care of the wound. I cleaned it with whiskey, an' seared it with a hot knife to stop the bleedin'."

Mary Burnet bent down and gently pressed around the hole in Pia's shoulder with her fingers, making Pia groan and wince in her sleep. "It appears you did just what was needed, Mr. Blue, but now it looks like there could be some infection."

"Yes, ma'am, those were my thoughts, too, but I don't see no pus yet an' that's a good sign, ain't it?"

Mary acted a bit surprised by his knowledge of wounds. "Mr. Blue . . ."

"Excuse me, Mrs. Burnet, but my full name's William Jackson Blue, although most folks just call me Billy."

"All right, Billy. Would you go to the house and ask Melissa to bring me some mustard root, lard, and clean cloths out of the cupboard?" She looked past Billy's shoulder to Juan, who was standing with his sombrero in his hand just inside the door. "Juan, please start a fire in the stove and bring me a pot to boil some water in. We've got lots of work to do if we're going to save this girl."

While Juan began to build a fire, Billy ran to the ranch house, bursting through the door without bothering to knock. Melissa Burnet was sitting at the kitchen table, drinking coffee while reading the Wichita Falls newspaper.

At his abrupt entrance she flinched in surprise, spilling coffee down the front of her white shirt. "Damn!" she exclaimed, irritation showing on her face. She jumped up and wiped away the stain with a towel, glaring through slitted eyes at Billy. "Around here, we generally knock before barging into someone else's house, Mr. Blue!"

Billy spread his hands wide, a chagrined expression on his face, thinking, It don't look like this one smiles overly much, or has much use for ranch hands. "Sorry 'bout that, Miz Burnet, but your mother sent me to fetch mustard root, lard, an' some clean cloths to treat Pia's shoulder. She said to tell you they was in the cupboard."

Melissa shook her head angrily. "I know where they are, Mr. Blue. You run on back there and tell Mama I'll bring them right over."

When she didn't move, still wiping at her shirt, Billy said, "She . . . she said we had to hurry, ma'am."

Melissa gave him a stare, eyes flat and dangerous looking, making Billy take a couple of steps backward, something no man had ever been able to make him do. "Get out, Blue!" she snapped. "I'll be there when I'm good and ready!"

"Yes, ma'am," Billy said, whirling around and stalking out the door as fast as his legs would carry him. Damn, he thought on the way back to the bunkhouse, I've seen friendlier rattlesnakes. I figure I'm gonna earn that hundred a month even if I don't come up against any rustlers.

When he got back, Mary was tending to Pia. She asked him if Melissa was coming.

He hesitated. "Well, ma'am, I gave her your message, but she was a mite put out that I asked her to hurry."

Mary looked up, another small smile tugging her lips. "Oh, I suspect she'll get over it, Billy. Now, hand me that knife I see on your belt. I need to cut some of this dress away where dried blood has made it stick to her skin."

As they worked to clear an area around the wound, Melissa sauntered in, arms full of mustard greens, cloths, and a tin of lard. When she saw the extent of Pia's injuries, her face blanched and she quickly stepped to her mother's side. "Goodness, Mr. Blue," she said, sounding apologetic now, looking at Billy with a concerned expression, "you didn't tell me she was hurt so badly."

Mary said to Melissa, "His name is William Jackson Blue, Melly."

"Well, William, why didn't you say it was this bad?" Melissa asked as she began to break up mustard greens and drop them in the water boiling on the camp stove.

"Uh, you didn't exactly ask, Miz Burnet," he answered, wanting to add, *nor show much concern for the squaw's condition at all,* but he figured that would just get her madder at him than she already was.

After the greens boiled for ten minutes, Mary took the thick liquid and poured it over a folded cloth, and gently laid it over Pia's wound. Pia arched her back and hissed through her teeth.

"Juan, you and Billy hold her arms. I don't want her moving until I've got this poultice applied just right."

While they held her, Mary scooped out large globs of lard in her hand and smoothed it over the cloth, patting it until the whole thing was smooth. "This mustard plaster will help keep the infection down, I hope," Mary said. "We'll send for the doctor over at Wichita Falls in the morning. With all the buffalo hunters and scoundrels around there, he's fairly expert at treating bullet wounds."

She stood and wiped her hands on her jeans. "Melissa, I've ruined her dress. Would you see if you have an extra one, or at least some pants and a shirt we could put on her?"

"But . . ."

Mary looked at Melissa, steel in her eyes and manner. "No buts, young lady. Do it right now!"

Melissa dropped her eyes, "Yes, ma'am," she said and walked out of the room, neck glowing red from embarrassment.

Mary shrugged, tilting her head to the side. "I'll ask you to excuse Melissa's feelings toward Indians, Billy. When she was little, no more that a girl, her older brother, Sam, was killed in an Indian raid on the ranch." She looked at Juan, "Those were wilder days," she added, and there was a trace of sorrow in her voice.

"*Sí,* señora, much different. We were the only ranch for a hundred miles. The Indians did not care too much for us to be here."

"I can understand that, ma'am," Billy said. "I ain't never lost no family to Indians, but I figure they're just like white folks, some good an' some bad. I try to judge 'em one at a time, but I can sure see where your daughter would have a hard time doin' that."

Mary smiled, reaching up to pat Billy's shoulder. "Why, Billy, I do believe you have the makings of a true gentleman."

Billy gave her a horrified look. "Oh no, ma'am, please don't hang that handle on me. I ain't no gentleman, I'm just a cowboy same as most folks around these parts."

Mary had an oddly serious look on her face. "I think there's much more to you than that, Billy, and I'm known as a right smart judge of character." She glanced over at the door, where Melissa was standing, a pile of shirts and pants in her arms. "Now, you men get. We've got to put some decent clothes on this young woman, and I want to make some soup and try to get her to eat it. She's going to need plenty of nourishment to keep the infection away and to heal herself."

Billy nodded, and put his arm around Juan's shoulders. "Come on, Juan, we need to do some serious jawing 'bout what we're gonna do about these rustlers been plaguing Mr. Burnet."

On the way to the big ranch house, Juan took a crumpled cigarillo out of his shirt pocket and screwed it into his mouth, striking a lucifer on his pants to set it on fire. As he exhaled a cloud of foul-smelling smoke, he glanced at Billy out of the corner of his eye. "Señor Billy, are you plenty good with gun?"

Billy gave a half smile. "I don't rightly know, Juan. I fought a lot a years in the war, an' I came out with my skin intact, so I guess I'm not too bad. Why do you ask?"

"Because the hombres you going up against are *muy pellagra,*" Juan said through teeth clenched on his cigar, "very dangerous men. Their *jefe* is called Cherokee Bill, and he is a bad *buscadero,* what you *Americanos* call *pistoleer*. He is said to have killed over twenty men, and he is not more than twenty years."

Billy nodded, still thinking about Juan's question of how good he was with his guns. He really didn't know . . . He was still unsure of how he had been able to beat Pickett to the draw, whether the famous gunman was drunk or hungover, sick, or just unlucky.

"They say," Juan continued, "last week Cherokee Bill shot a nine-year-old boy, just for watching him through a window." He dropped his cigar in the dust, shaking his head. "The *vaqueros* who ride with him are just as bad. Between them, they have killed many men."

"How come the law don't do anything about them?"

Juan shrugged. "The rangers are many miles away. By time they come, Bill and his *bandidos* are back in the Nations."

As they approached the porch of the ranch house, Billy

said, "By the way, I need some extra firepower. Does Mr. Burnet have any extra guns I can use?"

Juan smiled, showing yellow, tobacco-stained teeth. "*Sí.* Follow me."

He led Billy into the house, turned right, and entered a large study, with a stone fireplace on one wall and a large gun cabinet on the other.

Billy had never seen so many rifles and pistols outside of a gun shop. "Looks like he could start a war right here with all these weapons," Billy observed.

"You must remember, Billy, Señor Burnet started this *rancho* many years ago. We had to fight *los Indios, bandidos,* and even other ranchers to stay alive." The old Mexican grinned, his eyes vacant as he remembered his youth. "It was much exciting," he murmured, as if to himself.

Billy stepped up to the gun cabinet and opened its double doors. He took out a Sharps .50-caliber long rifle, another Winchester, a Greener 10-gauge double-barreled shotgun, and a brace of Army .44-caliber pistols, like the one he wore on his belt.

Juan raised his eyebrows. "Why you take the old *pistolas,* señor? The new Colts Peacemaker is much lighter, not make your hand so tired."

Billy held the Army pistol up. "See this barrel, Juan, it's two inches longer than the Peacemaker's is. That gives me an extra ten to fifteen yards of range. Also, the Peacemaker is a .45-caliber an' my Winchester an' Army are .44s. That means less ammunition I have to tote around." He shrugged. "Just seems to make sense to stay with what I'm used to shootin'."

Billy looked at a large Regulator clock on the mantel over the fireplace. "You up to takin' a little ride with me, Juan? It's 'bout time for the dog watch on the herd, an' I'd kinda like to look around and get acquainted with the punchers you got out there, so's they'll know who I am an' not take no potshots at me.''

Juan glared at Billy through slitted eyes. ''Of course Juan can still ride . . . You think maybe he is too old?''

Billy laughed. ''Hell no, pardner. Let's jingle our spurs.''

TWELVE

Billy climbed on his chestnut gelding, while Juan struggled up onto a dun that looked to Billy to be nearly as old as the vaquero. By the way his face wrinkled in pain, Billy knew riding a saddle bothered the old man's knees. Billy rode away from the barn at a slow lope, trying to make it as easy on Juan as he could.

As they approached a small herd of grazing longhorns, a Mexican and a black cowboy turned their horses to face them, hands falling toward pistols until they recognized Juan. Billy and the old man rode up to the pair of herd riders.

Juan introduced the men to Billy. "This is Luis Maldonado and Lincoln Jones, Señor Billy. Compadres, this is Billy Blue. Señor Burnet sent him to help us with Cherokee Bill and his *bandidos*."

Luis nodded, peering at Billy from under his hat brim. "Hello, señor."

Lincoln Jones frowned, glancing from Billy to Juan. "You mean to tell me Mr. Burnet only sent one man?" He leaned to the side to spit a stream of tobacco juice from a cud bulging in his cheek. "Hell, Cherokee Bill's got better'n fifteen hardcases ridin' with him."

Juan shrugged. "Señor Burnet sent only Señor Blue. Maybe he think that enough to do the job."

Luis looked at Billy's saddle, decorated with the Sharps and Winchester rifles and the Greener 10-gauge express gun in boots, and a war bag tied to the saddle horn containing his two extra Army-model Colt .44s and several boxes of shells.

"Señor Burnet must think you plenty good to send you here alone," Luis said, staring at Billy.

"I reckon he thinks I can get it done, since that's what he's payin' me for."

Billy knew he had to earn the cowboys' trust, for they would be his only backup in case of trouble. If they didn't believe in him, they would cut and run, leaving him to face the outlaws alone. He looked the men over, wondering if they would be of any help to him if he had to face trained gunmen. Luis was small, even for a Mexican, and appeared to be in his forties, old for a cowboy. Lincoln, on the other hand, was one of the biggest men Billy had ever seen, looking to be over six feet tall, with skin so black it was almost blue. Both men wore pistols and carried rifles in saddle boots, although Billy knew that didn't mean they knew how to use them against other men.

"You men had any trouble lately?" he asked.

Luis glanced at Lincoln, then back at Billy. "Well, there was this bunch of riders on south end of ranch earlier . . ."

Lincoln said, "Yeah, 'bout five or six men ridin' along like they was lookin' things over."

"Cherokee Bill with 'em?"

"No, but I thought I saw Jim French an' Sam McWilliams. Both of them been known to ride with Cherokee on occasion."

Billy stared at Burnet's cowhands, bewildered. "If you saw riders over to the south, what are you doin' here on the east side?"

Luis held out his hands. ''Señor Burnet gave us orders . . . He say if many outlaws come for us to leave. He not want us dead. He say is better to lose a few head than his last two cowboys.''

Juan nodded. ''Luis is right, Señor Billy. This is what the *patron* say. With most hands on trail drive, Señor Burnet just want us watch herd, not fight *bandidos.*''

Billy pulled his hat down tight. ''I think I'll just mosey on over to the south and take a look. Juan, why don't you go on back to the ranch house and see how Pia's doin'?''

Juan pulled a new Peacemaker Colt from his holster. ''I think I come with you, señor. There be too many for one man.''

Billy noticed the pistol still had traces of factory grease on the barrel, showing it hadn't been used yet. Hell, he thought, with his poor eyesight, Juan would be more dangerous to him than the outlaws. He smiled at Juan. ''No thanks. pardner, I'll take this little ride alone.''

Juan frowned, holstered his gun, and reined his dun horse in a tight circle to head back toward the ranch house.

Lincoln said, ''You sure you don't want help, Blue?''

Billy thought for a moment. He knew from experience most punchers weren't gunhands and fewer still had ever fired at another man in anger. On the other side of things, it wouldn't hurt to have the two men along to make his play look stronger.

''I'll tell you what, Lincoln. How about you and Luis follow me over to the south . . . show me where you saw these riders, and kinda stay behind me. Might be a show of force will be all it takes to get those hombres to cut an' run if they've got a notion to take cows that ain't theirs.''

''But, señor, what if they start shooting?'' Luis asked.

Billy shrugged. ''Like you said, Luis, you're not gettin' paid for this . . . I am. If any trouble starts I can't handle, you and Lincoln can hightail it back here to help Juan protect the ranch and the womenfolk."

Luis and Lincoln looked at each other, nodded, and followed Billy as he spurred the chestnut into a lope southward. The sun was disappearing to the west and the moon was not yet up, so the sky was blackening with gloom of dusk. As he rode, Billy inhaled a chestful of cooler night air, savoring without really thinking about it the sweet smell of honeysuckle vines, the piney tang of juniper trees in bloom, and the aroma of ever-present sage bushes. Soon, his nose wrinkled with the odor of burning flesh carried on a slight breeze. Someone's branding cattle, he thought, just as the three cowboys topped a ridge after a ride of four miles.

Billy reined to a halt, holding his hand up to silence Luis and Lincoln, as he stared down into a shallow valley below. He could see six men herding a small string of cattle there. Two seemed to be in charge, giving orders to the others on which beeves they wanted to take and which to leave behind. They had made a crude rope corral and one man was squatting next to a fire, heating a branding iron. A recently scorched calf was being led on a halter toward the corral.

Billy spoke over his shoulder without taking his eyes off the men below. "Those hombres work for Mr. Burnet?"

Lincoln answered, "No, sir. That there is Jim French," he said, pointing to a cowboy wearing a plaid shirt and black leather vest. "An' over there be Sam McWilliams," he added, showing Billy another man nearby, wearing a black shirt and no vest.

"Lincoln, give me a cut of that Durham's, would you?"

The black man, a surprised look on his face, cut a corner of chewing tobacco off his plug and handed it to Billy.

Billy chewed a couple of times, then parked the plug in his cheek as he shucked the Greener 10-gauge from its saddle boot and laid it across his saddle horn. He had found during the war that chewing tobacco during a firefight kept his mouth from going dry from fear, and in some strange way seemed to calm his nerves, as if the chewing gave him something to think about instead of his possible death.

"I'm gonna ease on down the ridge here an' come up behind them. I want you two to sit here on your horses with your rifles out and visible, so you can be seen from below." He turned his head and spit a brown stream into the dust. "If I go down, you two make tracks back to the ranch."

Both men nodded. Lincoln said, "Yes sir, Mr. Blue."

Billy smiled at that; he hadn't often been called mister before. He couldn't tell yet if he liked it or not. It seemed to him that killing a man was a poor way to earn respect.

Walking the chestnut down the ridge through thick brush, he began to think about how he was going to play it when he got to the men in the valley. He was outnumbered five, maybe six, to one. Not exactly the strongest hand he had ever been dealt. After considering his options, which weren't many, he decided on an aggressive offense, hoping that would make the outlaws pause, wondering what he was so confident about. Any hesitation on their part would give him an edge, and maybe that would be enough.

At the bottom of the ridge, he took a deep breath, squared his shoulders, and walked his horse forward out of the trees, hoping the men couldn't hear his heart beating wildly in his chest or see the fear-sweat beading on his forehead.

Jim French and Sam McWilliams were sitting on their horses, about ten feet from the man who was bending over a hog-tied cow and burning a brand into it with a running iron.

As the cow squirmed and grunted and smoke swirled into the air with an acrid odor of burning hair and flesh, Billy stopped his horse, held the Greener in his left hand, and eared back both hammers with a click that was loud in the quiet evening air.

French and McWilliams whirled around, their hands heading for their pistols. Billy noted out of the corner of his eye that the man with the branding iron wasn't armed, and the other three members of the gang were fifty yards away, still tending to the beeves in the corral.

"Howdy, gents," Billy drawled. He leaned to the side and spit juice on a small cactus. He held the Greener at a slight angle upward, not pointing directly at French and McWilliams, but not too far from it either. When they saw the scattergun, they stopped grabbing for their guns and held their hands still.

"Jesus, mister," French said, "you scared the hell out of us sneaking up on us like that." He gave a half grin at McWilliams. "Hell, we mighta shot ya."

Billy smiled back, trying to show he wasn't the least bit worried about that possibility. When he spoke, he tried to keep his voice low, hoping it wouldn't crack from fear. "Not likely," he said, and stared at the men as he spit again.

"Who are you, mister, and what're you doing out here this late at night?"

Billy didn't answer French's question. "I notice none of you gents is wearing spectacles, and I find that a mite strange."

French and McWilliams exchanged puzzled glances. "How's that, stranger?" McWilliams asked.

Billy lowered the Greener a mite, just to get their attention, and reached down and slowly loosened the hammer thong on the Walker at his hip. "Well, even from over here I can see those beeves're already wearin' 6666 brands. That's the Burnet brand if memory serves me, an' you gents don't work for Burnet."

"What business is it of yours?"

Billy shrugged, watching all six men out of the corner of his eye. The men over by the corral couldn't hear what they were saying, but so far they hadn't started to ride toward him and were out of range for a pistol shot, so he was able to give his full attention to the three in front of him.

"I happen to work for Mr. Burnet. My name's Billy Blue, an' he hired me to kill any fools who try to rustle his stock. You men wouldn't happen to be rustlers, would you?" He spit again, looking the group over slowly and deliberately, his eyes narrow and mean, a slight questioning frown on his face. " 'Cause that'd mean I'll have to kill you."

French and McWilliams looked at Billy like he was crazy, then both gave a nervous laugh. "You must be plumb loco, Mr. Blue." French spread his arms out wide. "Look around you. We got six men to your one." The outlaw's voice changed, turning hard, like cold steel on an anvil. " 'Stead of comin' around here threatening us, you oughta hope we don't blast you outta that saddle."

Billy's gaze didn't waver for an instant, his eyes fixed firmly on French and McWilliams, the leaders of the group. Nothing would happen until they called the play. "Not likely," Billy drawled again, seemingly unconcerned, staring hard at the pair of outlaws in front of him.

Now French and McWilliams looked worried, glancing around to see if Billy had any men behind him or over to the side in the trees. Sweat began to bead French's forehead and run down his cheeks, glistening in the early moonlight. "What do you intend to do, try and take on all six of us by yourself?" he finally asked.

"Don't have no choice, less you'd like to throw down them hoglegs and give it up," Billy answered in a soft voice, knowing the time for action was near. His stomach seemed to turn over, and from the way his legs felt, he would have fallen if he had been standing instead of sitting.

He took a deep breath, readying himself for whatever would happen. He could feel his muscles tense and his neck swell, like a buck challenging another over a doe in heat.

French and McWilliams glanced at each other again, looking puzzled, then back at Billy. "Who did you say you was?"

"Name's Billy Blue."

French grinned, teeth white against a brown face. "Well, you got balls, I'll say that for you, Billy Blue."

French went for his gun, hand moving toward his hip.

Time seemed to slow for Billy, like molasses on a winter morning. He could see everything happening as if it were at half speed. He pulled both triggers on the Greener and it exploded in his hand, roaring and shooting flame a foot or more out of the barrels, slamming back into his left arm with the force of a mule kick, almost knocking him out of the saddle.

He saw French's shoulders and head explode and disappear in a red mist. McWilliams, caught by the second load, was spun around and blown off his mount, his right arm missing up to his shoulder.

The rustler on the ground dropped his running iron and sprinted away from Billy toward the men by the corral, yelling "God damn, God damn, help me . . . help me!"

Billy whirled the chestnut, tears in his eyes both from the pain in his left arm and the thick cloud of gunsmoke swirling around his head. He drew his Walker and began to walk his gelding toward the corral, taking his time. He was surprised to discover he was beginning in some perverse way to enjoy the action that had started. The three men from the corral spurred their mounts away from him, leaning over their horses' heads, drumming spurs into their ribs. Billy saw them glancing over their shoulders. The bandits were soon out of range for their short-barreled .45 Colts, although not one made any move to shoot at him.

Slowly, calmly, as if making sure of his aim, he raised his pistol. He thumbed back the hammer, sighted, and fired over their heads, sending five booming shots harmlessly high, but with a message, a message he wanted carried back to the Indian Nations and the man behind all this rustling.

The third rider reined in hard, stopping his horse next to the running man. He reached down and swung the exhausted cowboy up behind him, jerked his horse around with a frantic look on his face, and took off toward the north as fast as the bronc could run carrying double.

Billy lowered his pistol into his holster, figuring it'd be better to let the men escape back to the outlaws' camp. Maybe the name Billy Blue would mean something to them the next time they heard it.

He swiveled in his saddle, drawing the Walker again as he heard the sound of two horses riding hard out of the trees behind him. Billy relaxed when he saw it was only Lincoln and Luis.

The two hands reined in, staring at the downed men on the ground around the small camp fire. Lincoln removed his hat and sleeved sweat off his forehead. "Mary mother of Jesus, I never seen anything like that, Mr. Blue!" he exclaimed, his eyes round and white in reflected light from the fire.

Luis muttered in a low voice, "*Madre de Dios,*" and made the sign of the cross on his chest, watching McWilliams groaning and thrashing on the ground, blood spurting from his shattered, torn shoulder.

After a moment, the gunslick sighed and became still, open eyes staring blindly at eternity.

Lincoln turned his gaze to Billy. "You done kilt both of 'em, Billy. I swear, one minute you was talking, calm and gentle like, an' the next that old Greener was spittin' fire and blowin' men to hell and gone." He paused, then said, "I was watching real close, an' I never even seen you draw that pistol, it just kinda appeared in yore hand, quick as a rattler strikin'!''

Luis shook his head. ''Those poor *bastardos* never had a chance.''

Billy narrowed his eyes at the Mexican. ''Luis, my daddy always told me ridin' the owlhoot trail was a risky way to make a livin'. I aimed to show those galoots just how risky it was.'' He spit a stream of tobacco juice over the head of his horse onto McWilliams's chest. ''If they didn't want to pay the band, they shouldn't've called the dance.''

Lincoln said, ''I just couldn't believe my eyes. Them outlaws reachin' for their guns, an' you just sittin' there, calm as a judge, till you blowed 'em to pieces like shootin' cans off'n a fence!''

Billy leaned his head back, smelling the acrid odor of cordite and gunpowder mixed with the odor of blood and death lingering on the night air. He guessed he'd have to get used to smells such as this, if he was to continue to make his living as a gunman. He took a deep breath, trying to calm the hammering of his heart now that the immediate danger was over. He felt a slight nausea, but knew from previous experience it would soon pass.

He got down off his horse and walked to stand over the bodies of the men he had killed, knowing somehow he had to look into their faces. If he was going to do the deed, he had to be able to face the results and know he had done the right thing; otherwise, he was no different from Leon Pickett and others who killed without thinking about it. He knew, instinctively, that if the sight of men he killed ever ceased to affect him, if he quit caring about what he had done, he was lost as surely as if a bullet had pierced his heart and left him lying on the ground instead of his enemies.

After a moment, Billy climbed back up in the saddle and gently spurred the chestnut. He rode slowly back toward the Burnet ranch house, wondering if he had been brave, or just foolish, to take on six men by himself. He wondered briefly if his father would have been proud of him for his actions tonight. Probably not, he figured. He'd've laid it off to dumb luck.

Luis pulled up next to him. "Señor, are you not going to go see about the men you shoot?"

Billy spit the cud of tobacco out, grimacing at the bitter taste. "Why should I?" He looked across at Luis. "You think they're gonna steal any more beeves tonight?"

"But . . . but even *bandidos* deserve a decent burial."

Billy shrugged, settling his hat down on his head. "You want to tend to them, go ahead. I'd just as soon let the coyotes and wolves take care of 'em." He looked up at the moon, rising higher over in the east. "The smell of blood'll bring the night critters out soon now. They won't have to lie there long." Billy wiped tobacco juice off his chin, and said, "Course, you two might want to gather them steers up and take 'em back to the main herd, now that there don't seem to be nobody else that wants 'em."

Luis and Lincoln looked at each other, as if they didn't quite know what to make of this stranger.

THIRTEEN

The next morning, over scrambled eggs, pancakes, bacon, and coffee, Juan told Billy he was going to take the buckboard into Wichita Falls for supplies, and to fetch the doctor for Pia.

"How's she doin'?" Billy asked. Mrs. Burnet had moved the Indian woman into the ranch house, evidently not feeling it was proper to leave her in the bunkhouse with the cowboys.

"She is *mucho* better, but Señora Burnet still want the doctor to look at her."

When he was shaving earlier, Billy saw Juan and Pia sitting on the front porch of the ranch house. From what he could see, Juan was doing most of the talking, and every so often, Pia would laugh and lower her eyes shyly toward the old *vaquero*. Billy couldn't resist teasing Juan about his obvious interest in the Indian girl.

"I notice you been spendin' quite a bit of time jawin' with Pia." Billy raised his eyebrows, a grin tugging at the corners of his lips. "You two gettin' serious?"

Juan blushed a fiery red. "Oh no, señor. I am only being courteous to our guest."

Billy gave him a skeptical look, causing the old man to grin more widely than ever. "But, now that you say it, she is much prettier than the cook Marguerite, no?"

"Yeah, I can see where she'd set your britches on fire, you randy old coot, 'specially out here a hundred miles from any other females."

Juan hitched up his pants with an injured look. "Juan not so old, but randy . . . yes, that I will admit to."

Billy stuffed the last bite of pancake into his mouth, washed it down with coffee, and asked, "You mind if I tail along with you to town? There's some things I need to pick up."

"*Sí como no?* Why not?"

After hitching up the buckboard, Billy climbed onto his bay, declaring he would rather ride a saddle than the hurricane deck of a buckboard any day.

As they were heading away from the ranch, Juan glanced over at Billy. "Pia say you *loco en la cabeza*."

Billy looked puzzled. "That so? Why does she think I'm crazy?"

"She say you talk all time. Talk to horse, talk to rocks, talk to you self."

Billy laughed. "Well, I guess she's right . . . it is a little strange. Course, you got to be a little crazy to be a cowpoke in the first place."

As they traveled, he thought about what he had said. It was true, a cowboy's life was full of hardship—long hours in the saddle, eating trail dust, sleeping in the open, in rain and snow and sleet, pushing thousand-pound animals who weren't inclined to move a certain direction unless you forced them to. He smiled, remembering the good things, too—the friendship of other punchers, the taste of hot coffee after twelve hours on the trail, the stars in a black sky, the sound of coyotes and wolves singing to each other in moonlight, even the smell of horse sweat and saddle leather. I reckon, he thought, it all evens out in the long run, the good and the bad, the happy and the sad, and none of it matters nohow once you're planted, so you might as well get on with life and not worry overly much about any of it.

They pulled into Wichita Falls just before noon. Narrow, dusty streets were full of ragged, down-on-their luck cowhands, buffalo hunters who carried their stink with them wherever they went, wagons, mangy dogs, and scruffy-looking kids. Ol' Hoss, Billy thought to himself as he looked around at the small town, you've been in some mighty poor places in your life, but this has to be the bottom of the barrel.

As they made their way down the main street, it seemed to Billy as if every other business was a saloon or gambling hall. Half of them weren't buildings, merely wooden facades with canvas tents off the back and boards across sawhorses serving as bars.

Juan saw the scowl on Billy's face and laughed. "You not like this town, Señor Billy?"

Billy wagged his head. "Not enough so's you can tell it."

Juan nodded. "*Sí,* is pretty rough town. It began as place for buffalo hunters to sell skins. Pretty soon saloons came, then whorehouses . . ." He shrugged. "If this place stay long enough, maybe good people start to move in and will become real town."

Billy looked to the side at a cowboy, hunched over, hands on his knees, throwing up in the street. "I wouldn't count on that happenin' any time soon, Juan."

Juan pulled back on the reins, planting his foot against the brake lever. The buckboard ground to a halt in front of a two-story building with a sign on the front that said

"Mary's Place." Billy raised his smiled. "It's a mite early in the day for that, ain't it, pardner?"

Juan laughed. "No, señor, you misunderstand. The doctor, he live upstairs, in a room over saloon." He tied the reins to the brake handle and started to climb down.

"Hold on there, Juan. Let me go get the doc. You just sit easy an' let those knees of your's rest awhile." Billy stepped off the bay and walked into the saloon, glad for a chance to stretch his legs after the long ride in from the ranch. The bartender told him which room was the doctor's and he went up the stairs.

When the doctor opened his door, Billy took note of his bloodshot eyes and sour whiskey breath.

"Doc, Mrs. Burnet out at the 6666 ranch wants you to come. There's a girl out there been shot in the arm."

The doctor yawned. "All right. I'll get my things together and be right there." He rubbed his chin whiskers and looked longingly over his shoulder at a bottle of whiskey on his dresser.

Billy poked a stiff finger in the man's chest. "Doc, this particular woman is a friend of mine, an' I'd be plenty upset if anything bad were to happen to her . . .'specially if I found out you'd been drinkin' 'fore workin' on her. You understand what I'm sayin'?"

The doctor's eyes widened and he stepped back, fear on his face at the look Billy was giving him. "Why, yes sir, of course. I'll just shave and head right on out there."

Billy smiled and patted him on the shoulder. He looked pointedly at the whiskey bottle. "Don't stop to eat nor nothin', Doc. I'm sure Mrs. Burnet'll be glad to provide lunch for you."

He went back outside and mounted the gelding. "Now let's go get them supplies, Juan."

Juan drove the buckboard another hundred yards down the street and pulled up in front of a cedar-sided building that housed the local mercantile, and he and Billy went inside. While Juan got ranch supplies, Billy picked out twenty boxes of .44 shells, a case of dynamite and blasting caps and fuses, two cans of gunpowder, and extra .50-caliber cartridges for the Sharps.

"You fellers planning on goin' to war?" the shopkeeper asked cautiously.

"Only if the opportunity presents itself," Billy answered, making the man's expression darken.

The smell of the place again reminded Billy of home and childhood, and of his friend Asa Carter. On a whim, he reached into the candy jar on the counter and brought out a handful of peppermint sticks. He handed one to Juan, put one in his mouth, and stuck the others in the sack to take back to the ranch. He wondered if Pia had ever tasted peppermint, and if she would like it.

After they loaded the buckboard, Billy asked Juan if he thought Mr. Burnet would mind if he used some of his credit to buy some new clothes and such. "My toes are 'bout near comin' through these old boots."

Juan told him to go ahead, he could have Mrs. Burnet take it out of his pay come the end of the month. Billy picked out several shirts, a couple of pair of denims, and, most importantly, a pair of shiny, stovepipe black boots. When he was finished he asked Juan if he could buy him a drink, beer or whiskey.

"Certainly, señor. A man who turns down free whiskey is a fool, and I am very smart."

On the way to the saloon, Billy realized with a start that he hadn't needed whiskey to sleep for some time now, and his dreams of Jessie Small were no longer plaguing him, making him sweat, making sleep impossible. He thought back to the last time he had dreamed . . . It was the night before he shot Leon Pickett.

Could killing a man who desperately needed it have

cured him, or was it simply facing the possibility of his own death, the realization that it was eventually going to come, and the acceptance of that fact that had rid him of his night demons?

He didn't know, and he didn't much care what had done it. The fact was, he was no longer dependent on alcohol to get through the night. He sat a little straighter in his saddle, relieved somehow of a burden he hadn't known he was carrying, a weakness of spirit he was glad to be shed of.

Billy swung down and pushed through the saloon batwings, smiling to himself. It felt good to be coming for a drink not because he needed it, but merely because he wanted it.

He and Juan walked to the bar and ordered whiskeys. Before the bartender could set their drinks down, a drunken voice called from behind them, "The only thing stinks more'n a buff'lo hunter is a Mexican."

Billy felt Juan stiffen beside him, but the old man did not turn around, merely hunching his shoulders as he turned to leave.

"That's right, señor, why don't ya go on down the street to the cantina. That's where your kind belongs, not here with respectable white folks." It was the same man who spoke.

Billy put his hand on Juan's shoulder, holding him in place, then calmly poured both of them jiggers of whiskey. He touched Juan's glass with his, raised it to his lips and drank it down in one motion, then he slowly turned to look at the man doing all the talking.

Billy could feel the familiar weakness in his knees, the cold, hollow feeling in the pit of his stomach, and wondered again if he was being brave, or just foolish.

"You got something to say, mister, why don't you say it to me, 'stead of to a man old enough to be your father . . . 'ceptin' he had more sense than to bed your mother."

A young, belligerent man who appeared to Billy to be about eighteen or nineteen years old pushed back his chair and jumped to his feet. He held his right hand out from a pistol tied down low on his leg. "I'm gonna dust you through and through fer sayin' that, mister."

Billy leaned back, elbows on the bar, his face calm, as if he didn't have a care in the world. He gave the gunslick a half smile that didn't reach his eyes. "Not likely," he said, voice low and husky. He reached down with a deliberate motion to unhook the rawhide hammer thong on his Army .44. Without taking his eyes off the man, he straightened and stood up, knees slightly bent, leaning a little at the waist.

"All right, big mouth. All you're doing so far is flappin' your jaws. You gonna talk me to death or pull that iron you got strapped to your leg?" The words came out of Billy's mouth as if someone else was saying them. He wasn't consciously trying to goad the man into a fight. He remembered his dad, just prior to one of his many whippings, telling Billy his smart mouth was going to get him killed one day. Billy wondered briefly if today was that day.

"You threw your chips in this pot, boy, an' it's time to call the bet or fold your hand," Billy snapped.

The teenager's face flushed and he flexed his fingers, ready to draw. Suddenly, a man at the same table snapped his fingers and said, "Shit . . . you know who that is, Ozark?"

The young man hesitated, eyes flicking to the side for a second, then back to Billy. "No. Tell me who this bastard is so we'll know what to put on his grave marker."

"That there's Billy Blue. He's the one let Leon Pickett make the first move and drilled him 'fore he could clear leather."

The young man's face blanched white and he stiffened,

now holding his hand out away from his gun. "That true, mister? Is you Billy Blue?"

"Yeah, I'm Billy Blue. Who are you?"

"I'm Ozark Jack Berlin. I've got a warrant out on me an' I'm headed up into the Nations to join up with Cherokee Bill. You wanna come along? I hear he can use good men like you."

Billy's lips curled, but his eyes remained cold as winter ice on a pond. He glanced at Juan, then back at Ozark Jack. "I think you owe my pardner here an apology."

Ozark Jack frowned and hesitated, as if considering his chances of taking Billy. After a moment he relaxed his gun hand and walked over toward the bar. "Why sure, I didn't know he was with you. I'm sorry, señor. I didn't know you was Billy's partner. No offense."

Juan's eyes glittered hate, and he leaned forward to spit on Jack's boots, then he turned his back and began to sip his whiskey.

Billy shrugged. "I guess you and your friends better be on your way. It's a long ride to the Nations."

"Yeah, well, we was about finished here anyway." He waved to his companions. "Come on, men. Time we moved on." Looking again at Billy, he asked, "You sure you don't want to ride with us?"

"No, but give Cherokee Bill a message for me, will you?"

"Sure."

"Tell him if he raids the Burnet spread again, I'm gonna kill him—him and any other bastard that rides with him."

"What . . . ?"

"You heard me, Ozark Jack." Billy made a face as he said the words, as if the name left a bad taste in his mouth. "Tell him I'll do to him what I did to Jim French and Sam McWilliams last night. I'll plant him forked end up and leave his carcass for the coyotes."

Ozark Jack frowned, as if he couldn't believe what he was hearing. "You say you kilt Jim and Sam last night?"

Billy didn't answer, merely nodded, his eyes on Ozark Jack's right hand.

"Well, were it a fair fight?" the young tough asked.

"The odds were about right—six of them, and one of me. But if Cherokee Bill or any of his men come on the Burnet spread again, they can ask those boys themselves, when they see 'em in Hell."

Ozark Jack opened his mouth, as if to say something, but the look in Billy's eyes must have made him change his mind. He pulled his hat on and whirled toward the batwings without a backward glance.

Billy had turned back to the bar and picked up his whiskey, when he caught a sudden movement out of the corner of his eye. He grabbed for his Walker, but before his hand touched the handle, a chair crashed against his back, knocking him to the floor.

A bulky man with a wild look in his eye was standing over Billy, broken remnants of a chair in his hands.

"I cain't allow you to talk to my friend Ozark like that, Blue. I don't care how good you are with that hogleg, I'm gonna beat you to death with my bare hands."

Billy looked up from the floor to see a giant of a man standing over him. Jesus, Billy thought as he shook his head, trying to clear it. He looks damn near seven feet tall.

The cowboy stood there, opening and closing his fists, drool dripping from the corner of his mouth, as if he wasn't quite right in the head. "Git up, Billy Blue, I'm gonna kill you."

Billy had started to reach for his Walker, when Ozark Jack called from across the room. "Don't do it, Blue." He had a pistol in his hand, pointing it at both Billy and Juan. "Let's keep this a fair fight. Johnny there ain't heeled, 'cept with his fists."

A loud double click sounded from behind the bar. The bartender had an American Arms double-barreled 12-gauge express gun aimed at the entire room. "That goes for you, too, Ozark. I allow fisticuffs in my place, but I don't allow no gunplay. If anybody pulls a trigger, I'll blast 'em to hell and worry about the windows later."

While the man Ozark called Johnny was distracted, Billy drew back his foot and kicked him in the knee as hard as he could with the heel of his boot. The big man howled and doubled over, and Billy jackknifed his foot again, planting the toe of his boot under the man's chin and knocking him backward over a table, spilling beer, whiskey, and poker chips all over the floor.

Billy scrambled to his feet, gingerly feeling the knot on the back of his head. He felt sure the fracas was over. He heard what sounded like a grizzly's growl and turned just in time to see Johnny throw the table aside like it weighed nothing. His jaw was hanging crooked and was obviously broken, but it didn't seem to faze the crazed man. He opened his arms wide and walked toward Billy, his eyes bulging, blood dripping from his mouth.

Billy set his feet, and when Johnny got close enough, he hit him with all his might in the middle of his face, shattering his nose. It didn't even slow Johnny down. He shook his head once before he grabbed Billy, picked him up over his head, and threw him across the bar, sending him crashing to the floor.

Billy lay there a moment, among shattered glass and stale beer, wondering if the man was truly going to kill him. Damn, hoss, he thought dully, still in a daze, you come through a war and several shooting matches and now some galoot in a saloon is fixing to beat you to death.

He put his hands on the bar to pull himself up, and saw something that might save his life. Billy grabbed the handle of a keg buster, a wooden sledgehammer, and stood up.

Johnny leaned across the bar, hamlike hands reaching for Billy's throat. Billy didn't hesitate. He brought the keg buster down in a roundhouse swing square on the top of Johnny's head.

Johnny stopped reaching and stood there for a moment, then his eyes crossed and he fell straight backward to land with a loud thud on the wooden floor.

While Ozark Jack and his men were watching their friend fall, Billy drew his Walker and laid it on the bar, his hand on the handle. "You gents want to take that trash with you when you leave, or you want me to finish what he started?" Billy asked as he thumbed back the hammer on his .44.

Ozark Jack's face paled. He evidently knew he didn't stand a chance of bringing his gun up before Billy could plug him. He slowly took his finger off the trigger and placed the pistol in his holster.

Glaring at Billy, he motioned two of his men to pick Johnny up. "Maybe we'll see each other again, Blue."

"If we do, I'll be the last thing you see this side of Hell, Jack."

Ozark Jack and his men walked through the batwings, two of them dragging Johnny, as he was too heavy to lift.

After a moment, Billy heard them ride off down the street. He didn't know if he was relieved there was no gunplay, or disappointed. On the one hand, he wasn't a bloodthirsty killer, anxious to notch his gun and shoot another man, but then again, he still wasn't quite sure if he was really good or had been just lucky so far.

He turned back to the bar, and felt Juan staring at him. "You did not have to defend me or fight for me, Señor Billy. Juan can take care of himself."

"Of course you can, Juan," Billy said, slapping him on the shoulder, "but that's what partners are for, to help each other out once in a while."

"Oh, in that case is okay. I buy you whiskey now, 'pardner.' "

After downing another slug of whiskey, Juan glanced at Billy out of the corner of his eye. "May I ask you something, Señor Billy?"

"Sure, Juan."

"Does it bother you to kill men, like the gunfighter Leon Pickett, and those mens at the *ranchito* last night?"

Billy paused, his glass halfway to his lips. He considered what Juan asked him, not having thought overly much about it one way or the other. He finished his drink and turned to Juan. "Juan, to tell you the truth, I don't rightly know. My pa always told me it was wrong to kill a man, 'cept in war or if'n he was to draw down on you first." He signaled the barkeep to bring them another round. "All I know is, Leon Pickett didn't give me no choice in the matter. It was either draw and kill him or he was gonna kill me, so that one don't bother me none a'tall."

He picked his glass up after it was filled and drank it down in one long swallow. "The men on the ranch, I reckon that's another matter. I was hired on by Mr. Burnet to protect his stock, an' to go after the men who rustled his cattle if I get the chance." He shrugged. "Last night, those men were breakin' the law, committin' a hangin' offense. I figure I just did my job an' saved the county the price of a trial an' a necktie party."

"What about leaving those *hombres* without a Christian burial?"

Billy shrugged again. "Hell, Juan, wolves and coyotes got to eat, too, same as worms. I don't figure it made much difference to those owlhoots one way or t'other." He threw some money on the counter and looked at Juan. "That about all your questions? I done talked more the last two days than the previous six months."

"*Sí,* señor. Let us *vamanos a la ranchito.* We don't want to miss supper."

As Juan struggled up on the buckboard and Billy climbed into the saddle, Billy looked back over his shoulder at the bar. "Juan, I got to remember to stay outta saloons." He shook his head as he walked the bay down the street. "Seems I always manage to find trouble in one."

FOURTEEN

Billy was just finishing trying on his new clothes in the bunkhouse when Juan came through the door.

"Señor Billy, the señora Burnet ask me to invite you to have supper in big house with her and the señorita."

Billy was surprised "Is that usual, Juan, for the hands to eat with the owners?"

"No, señor, is most strange." Juan grinned and made a face. "You must be *muy importante hombre,* eh?"

Billy smiled back. "You keep talkin' like that, Juan, an' I'm gonna plant these new black boots up alongside your rear end."

Juan held up his hands. "Okay, okay, señor, but you must hurry. The señorita, she not like to be kept waiting."

"I'll just bet she don't." Billy grabbed his hat, wiped his boots again on the back of his pants legs, and walked out the door. He moved slowly toward the ranch house, just to let Juan, and himself, know he wasn't afraid of Señorita Burnet.

He stepped up on the porch and took his hat off to smooth his unruly hair before he knocked on the door.

It was jerked open by Melissa Burnet, dressed for dinner in a bright blue gingham dress. "It's about time . . . ," she began, then stopped and looked him up and down. "Well, look who's dressed up like a sore toe. And I thought those clothes you showed up in were grown to your skin."

Billy's cheeks turned hot. "I asked Juan an' he said it'd be okay if I charged the new duds to the ranch. You can take it out of my first months wages." He paused, returning her look for a moment. "Now it looks like I'm gonna have to borrow some more money."

"And why is that?"

"I bet Juan a dollar against a biscuit you didn't own no dresses."

Her eyes narrowed for a moment, then she seemed to force a smile. "Come in, William. I can't wait for my mother to get a look at you."

As he followed her toward the dining room, Billy cursed her under his breath. He'd never met a more frustrating woman, or a prettier one, he thought, as he admired the way she filled out the gingham dress. It was the first time he had seen her in anything other than denims. Her hair was pulled up and pinned in a soft pile on top of her head, leaving her neck and shoulders bare. He had never seen skin so fair and soft, and found he couldn't take his eyes off her as she walked ahead of him.

Just before she got to the dining room, Melissa glanced back over her shoulder and saw where his eyes were glued. She stopped and glared at him, hands on hips, a flush spreading across her cheeks. "Why, I never . . . ," she began, until her mother called from the table, "Come in, Billy. Supper is ready and waiting."

Billy stepped through the door and nodded politely. "Evenin' Mrs. Burnet."

"Good evening, Billy. You look very nice tonight." She

pointed to an empty seat at the end of the table, where Melissa was already seating herself. "Have a seat. I believe supper is ready to be served."

Melissa glanced at him out of the corner of her eye and murmured, "Been ready for an hour now. Probably getting cold waiting . . ."

"Melissa!" Mary Burnet did not raise her voice, but Billy could hear steel in it as she rebuked her daughter. "Mr. Blue is a guest in our home, and he will be treated as such. Do you hear me?"

Melissa lowered her head to stare vacantly at her plate. "Yes, ma'am."

"Good. Then why don't you see if he would like some wine, or perhaps a cool beer?"

Melissa looked at Billy, and though her face and lips smiled, her eyes were hard, and he knew she blamed him for her mother's anger. "William, would you care for a drink, a glass of wine or beer?"

Billy struggled to keep his expression neutral and not to smile. "No, ma'am, but I'd appreciate some coffee if you have any."

Without taking her eyes off his, Melissa said, "Marguerite, would you bring Mr. Blue some coffee?"

After the elderly Mexican woman brought Billy a steaming cup of coffee, Mary gave instructions in fluent Spanish and the woman disappeared into the kitchen.

While Marguerite was putting platters of roast beef, mashed potatoes, and ears of boiled corn on the table, Mary asked Billy, "Do you mind if we discuss business while we eat?"

"Not at all, ma'am," Billy answered, surprised at the question.

"I have read over my husband's letter, and I want you to know that we all," and she gave Melissa a flat look, "appreciate how you've come to help us out in our time of need."

Billy nodded as she continued. "Juan tells me you've already had a run-in with rustlers, and . . . how did he put it . . . dispatched them nicely."

Billy speared a slab of roast beef and placed it on his plate, next to a large pile of mashed potatoes and two ears of corn. He picked up a roll, and had to bounce it back and forth in his hands when he found it was still hot. He noticed Melissa watching his antics, and felt his face blush with embarrassment.

He avoided looking at Melissa, and directed his gaze to Mrs. Burnet. "I hope you'll excuse my manners, Mrs. Burnet. I'm not used to eatin' in polite society, most of my meals bein' out on the trail."

Mary glared at Melissa. "Think nothing of it, Billy. My husband and I founded this ranch years ago, when we were the first white settlers within a hundred miles. In spite of what some people seem to think," and she fixed a withering stare on Melissa again, "we are not what you would call high society. We are simple ranchers, used to eating with cowboys and hired hands. You do not have to apologize for your manners, which, by the way, I think are just fine." She smiled at him, and then picked up an ear of corn with her hands and began to eat it as he would, from side to side.

"Thank you, ma'am." He, too, picked up some corn and began to eat it.

Melissa took her corn and used a knife to scrape the kernels off into a small pile on her plate, then daintily ate them with a fork.

Billy shook his head, wondering why Melissa hadn't joined in with her mother in trying to make him feel at home. He guessed she didn't much care how he felt, and he wished he could quit worrying about the impression he was making on her.

After a moment, he took a drink of coffee, sat back, and said, "Mrs. Burnet, last night was just the beginnin'. I doubt if losin' a couple of hands is goin' to do much to change Cherokee Bill's idea that your ranch is easy pickin's for him and his gang. Long as cattle prices are up and the Indians in the Nations need beef, he's gonna be on the prowl for any he can steal."

Mary nodded. "I'm sure you're right, Billy. What do you have planned for your next step?"

"My understanding is that Mr. Burnet wants me to see if I can pick up the trail of those cattle that have already been stolen, follow 'em to where the rustlers have 'em stashed, an' see if I can get the beeves back."

"But, Billy, we don't have any men to send with you after the rustlers." Mary spread her hands. "We barely have enough to keep what's left of the herd together as it is."

"Oh, I don't expect no help, ma'am. Mr. Burnet made it clear I was to go after them cattle on my own."

Melissa interrupted, exasperation in her voice. "William, you can't be serious! Luis said there were tracks of at least ten men in the gang. You can't mean to go after them all by yourself . . . You wouldn't have a chance."

Billy grinned. Could it be Melissa really cared what happened to him? "Well, Miz Burnet, I knew the odds when I signed on for the job." He shrugged. " 'Sides, I ain't exactly plannin' on ridin' up to the whole gang of *bandidos* an' drawin' down on 'em. In spite of how it might look, I am a mite smarter'n that."

Mary said, "Just what do you plan to do, Billy?"

"I figure to get what information I can from Luis and Lincoln about the bandits, then I'm gonna trail 'em to wherever it is they go to. Once I find their hideout, or their main camp, I'll decide then how to handle the situation . . . whether to try to hit an' run, in a way of speakin', like Quantrill an' his men did durin' the war."

Melissa spoke. "You are forgetting one thing, William. Bill Quantrill had over two hundred men riding with him; he wasn't a lone cowboy with an over-inflated opinion of himself who thought he could defeat an entire army." She looked at her mother. "Men!" she said under her breath, and threw down her napkin, storming out of the room without another word.

Billy watched her leave. "What do you suppose put such a burr under her saddle?" he asked quietly.

Mary looked at him, a bemused smile on her lips. "Why, Billy, if I didn't know better, I'd think she was concerned for your safety."

Billy chuckled. "I doubt that. She don't even like me."

Mary shook her head. "Billy, you really don't know anything about women, do you?"

Billy turned his attention back to his roast beef. "I guess not, ma'am, but then I ain't never met nobody like Miz Melissa before."

Mary muttered in a voice she didn't think Billy could hear, "Nor she you, Billy."

After supper with the Burnets, Billy saddled up the bay and persuaded Juan to ride out to the spot where Luis and Lincoln had their night camp. It wasn't much of a ride, less than half an hour until they sighted a twinkling fire. He and Juan rode into camp after announcing themselves with the cry "Burnet riders!"

He squatted next to their camp fire and spread out a surveyor's map Mary Burnet had given him on the dirt in front of Lincoln and Luis.

"Luis, I hear it was you who first found the tracks of

the rustlers. Can you show me on this here map which way they led?''

Luis studied the map, puffing on a battered cigar and taking an occasional sip from a tin cup of coffee. After a moment, he pointed a stubby finger at the map. ''They took off towards the north-northwest.'' He leaned forward and stretched his hand out. ''Right about here they crossed Sullivan's Creek and kept on going straight north.'' He looked up into Billy's face. ''The land up that way gits real rocky, lots of cactus and piñon trees, and it's thick with mesquite bushes.'' He shook his head. ''Pretty soon after that, I lost the trail, but I figure they headed on up into the Nations.''

''How'd you know it was Cherokee Bill's gang what done it?''

Juan spoke up. ''His men come often into Wichita Falls to sport with womens there. They make no secret they spending moneys got from Señor Burnet's cattle.'' He shrugged. ''I stay small, like mouse, in corner of saloon and hear many things. They also say they intend to take more of Señor Burnet's cattle until he comes back from Kansas.''

Billy pursed his lips, thinking. ''Tell me more 'bout this Cherokee Bill. I heard some talk 'bout him in a saloon once, how he was a pretty bad *hombre,* but I don't know no particulars.''

Juan pulled a pair of stogies from his shirt pocket, and after giving one to Billy, he struck a lucifer on his pants leg and lit them both. As a cloud of pungent blue smoke swirled around his head, he said, ''It will be better coming from Lincoln, Billy. He knows many other Negro cowboys, and Cherokee Bill is somewhat of a hero to them, and they tell their stories to Lincoln.''

''Lincoln, tell me what you know,'' Billy said.

Lincoln cut a piece of tobacco off his plug of Durham's,

chewed for a moment to get it just right, then began to talk. "Cherokee Bill's real name's Crawford Goldsby, and he hails from Fort Concho, Texas. His mother was half-Cherokee and half-Negro, his father was all Negro. When he was a baby, still on his mama's tit, his father killed some buff'lo hunters while he was in the army. When the Rangers come to 'rest him, he ran off to the Nations to hide out. Soon after that, his mama ran off, too, and Crawford was pretty much left to fend for hisself." Lincoln paused to spit into the fire, causing it to crackle and hiss.

"When he was 'bout eighteen, he shot another Negro after the man beat the shit out of him. He left town one jump ahead of the sheriff and went into hiding, then he joined up with two other bandits, Jim and Bill Cook."

Luis interrupted, "They both be breeds, part Cherokee an' part pure devil."

"They Negro men, too?" Billy asked.

Lincoln nodded, "Leastways part black, an' part who knows?"

Juan flipped his cigar butt into the camp fire. "That's when he took up the name Cherokee Bill," he said and glanced at Billy to see if he wanted to hear the rest. "They formed what was to be called the Cook gang, riding with Bill Cook, Cherokee Bill, Lon Gordon, Sam McWilliams, Henry Munson, Curtis Dayson, and others."

Lincoln said, "You met up with McWilliams the other night, an' he's the one whose arm you shot off."

"What did this Cook gang do?" Billy asked. He held out his cup and Lincoln poured some steaming coffee into it from the pot on the fire.

Juan shrugged. "Almost everything badmen can do. Robbed banks, railroads, stages, killed womens and childrens, and raped those they didn't kill."

Luis said, "Every time the Rangers take off after them, they hightail it back to the Nations. It's said even the Cherokee authorities are afraid to go up against him and his gang.''

''You have any idea whereabouts they may hole up?''

Juan glanced at Billy through narrowed eyes. ''Señor Blue, please give up this plan to go after Cherokee Bill. Señor Burnet will understand if you say there are too many *bandidos* for one man. Stay here with Luis and Lincoln and Juan and maybe they will not steal any more cattle . . . That is enough for you to do.''

Billy stared down into his cup, as if the steam might have some message for him. He thought about what Juan was saying. Sure, a hundred dollars a month was a goodly sum, but it wouldn't do him no good if he got killed 'fore he could earn it. On the other hand, he did give the man his word he'd try an' get his beeves back for him.

He glanced back to Juan. ''I know what you're sayin', Juan, an' I 'preciate the thought, but I hired on to do a job, an' wishin' it were easier don't get it done, nor earn my pay.''

He stood and dusted off the seat of his jeans. ''I figure I'll just have a mosey on up into the Nations, follow those cattle tracks as far as I can, an' see what develops.'' He pitched the remainder of his coffee into the fire. ''Hell, it might be I can't find no *bandidos* to kill.''

Lincoln shook his head, his eyes wide and white in the moonlight. ''I don't think you're gonna have any trouble finding no outlaws in the Nations, Billy. They be plumb thick as fleas on a hound dog up thataway . . . No, your problem's gonna be getting out of there without your top-knot decoratin' one of their lodge poles.''

Billy's face became hard. ''Takin' it may be harder'n those galoots think.'' He walked over to where his horse was ground-reined. As he stepped into the saddle, he tipped his hat to the three men still squatting by the fire. ''I thank you gents for your help. I'll be leavin' at first light an' I'll see you when I get back."

As he rode back toward the ranch house to get a few hours' sleep, he heard Luis say in a soft, sorrowful voice, "You mean *if* you get back."

FIFTEEN

Billy squinted against the rising sun as he checked the horizon to the north for clouds. He didn't want to start his trip after Cherokee Bill and the stolen beeves if a spring storm was coming. The sky was clear, with only scattered orange and yellow clouds reflecting morning light. The air was cool and crisp, and he could almost taste sage blossoms he scented on soft morning breezes from the west.

He stood next to his horses, giving his packing a final check. Since his bay gelding was heavy-barreled and thick through the chest, he decided he would use it for his packhorse. The chestnut was narrow through the croup and long-backed, with slender legs giving it both initial speed and great bottom and endurance, and he elected to ride it. He knew that as long as he kept it grain-fed and sound on all four feet, no one would be able to catch him or run him down, in the event he had to flee for his life. Billy believed, as most cowboys did, that grass was fine for horse fodder, but grain was essential when it came to stamina.

Considering the danger he was riding into, Billy had the bay carrying a saddle in addition to provisions. He had heard of more than one cowboy dying from being left afoot.

He had borrowed an old Mexican-style saddletree from Juan and covered it with a loose rawhide covering the *vaquero* called a *mochila*. Juan advised him this was the lightest saddle he could use to minimize the weight the bay would be carrying.

He put most of his extra ammunition and food in saddlebags; then added his lariat, tie-rope, slicker, bedroll, grain for the horses, and two large canteens filled with water. He also put the Sharps Breechloading Sporting rifle he had found in Mr. Burnet's gun case on the bay, since it weighed nine pounds and he wanted to keep the chestnut's load as light as possible.

He slung his bag containing extra .44 shells and two additional Colt Army .44s over the chestnut's saddle horn, and also long-gun slings for his Winchester rifle and Greener 10-gauge shotgun, since rifle boots under the saddle skirts would chafe the gelding too much on the long ride.

When he was satisfied, he looked at Juan and clasped his hand. ''Thanks for the help, pardner.''

''*Vaya con dios, compadre,*'' Juan answered, his eyes troubled. ''I hope this is not last time I see you, Señor Billy.''

''Not likely,'' Billy answered, with a grin he had to force. He wasn't at all sure he would come back from this little jaunt, but he knew it was something he had to do. Otherwise he'd never know the answer to questions plaguing him since he stood over Leon Pickett, staring down into his dead eyes. Was he brave, or just foolish and lucky? Hell, his pappy had always told him he was too stubborn for his own good; maybe this trip would prove the old man right after all.

''You sure you want no help? Juan is ready to ride with you if you desire,'' the old man said with a wistful look in his eyes.

"I was raised to believe a man has to saddle his own horses and kill his own snakes. Mr. Burnet's payin' me good wages for this job, an' I intend to earn it."

He reined the chestnut around, tugged on the dally rope to the bay, and began to walk his mounts north. As he passed the ranch house, he saw Melissa standing in the window, still in her nightshirt, hair mussed, face blotchy from sleep. Ol' hoss, that's about the most beautiful woman I ever seen, he thought.

She reached down, pulled the window open, and called out to him. "William Jackson Blue, you be careful and ride with your guns loose. I expect you to live long enough to earn the money we paid for those fancy duds you charged to us, you hear?"

Billy frowned. Why bless my soul, Billy, he thought, I do believe Miss Melissa is startin' to care if you live or die. Now that's a notion worth hangin' on to.

Billy tipped his hat and gave her a wink, which evidently infuriated her for she blushed deeply and slammed the window down almost hard enough to crack the glass. Damn, Billy thought, that she-wolf would probably put that broken glass down on my wages, too. He shook his head. *Women! Damned if I'll ever understand 'em.*

"Horse," he muttered to the chestnut, "I swear you're lucky you been cut. You don't have to worry 'bout chasing no fillies around, wonderin' what kinda tricks they're goin' to play on you next. All you got to think about is what kinda trouble this crazy cowboy ridin' your back is gonna get into next."

He picked up the trail of the stolen cattle a couple of miles north of the valley where he shot and killed the rustlers. These outlaws were so sure of themselves, they didn't even seem to make any attempt to cover their tracks.

"Horse, that don't look too good. Anybody ain't afraid

of bein' tailed must have good cause to be so damn brave. I may be takin' you and your bay friend back there into more trouble than I can handle."

He rode along the tracks, taking his time and conserving his mounts' energy. As he rode, he sang an off-key version of a song called "Cantina Santa Fe," causing the chestnut to look back at him once when he hit a particularly sour note. "Singin' never was my specialty," he muttered, explaining his lack of musical talent to an animal . . . a sure sign he was losing his senses, should anyone but another cowboy overhear him. One-sided conversations with a horse occurred as a result of loneliness on long trail drives, and it was something a cowhand understood.

As he got farther from the ranch, and friendly territory, he became more careful, riding slower and checking large open ranges before venturing across them. While he wasn't truly expecting an ambush on this side of the Red River, it paid to be careful in unfamiliar country. Thus he traveled this way until dusk, always being sure of his surroundings before riding out in plain sight.

He built a small fire, surrounding it with large stones so it wouldn't throw off much light, and boiled coffee. While it was bubbling, he walked to the bay and reached into the saddlebag containing his food, intending to grab a little jerky and a cold biscuit or two. To his surprise, he found a sack containing a half dozen bearclaws, sugary donuts that might have been put there by Melissa. The idea that she could have made them especially for him put Billy's mind onto thoughts that would make his sleep restless.

Dawn found him in the saddle on the trail of Burnet's stolen cattle. Juan and Luis had been right—the hoofprints led due north toward the Nations and Cherokee Bill's reputed hideout. It was no surprise. Indian Territory had become a roost for plenty of wanted men—about as dangerous a place for a man who couldn't defend himself as any Billy knew of. He was headed for a test of his gunmanship if he ran across Cherokee Bill and his gang. And deep inside, he hoped he wasn't biting off a mouthful he couldn't chew.

After another full day in the saddle, Billy finally crossed the Red, shallow this time of year but always full of tricky quicksand beds, onto the reservation known as the Indian Nations. It was stark, dry, almost worthless land, with alkali dust blowing on winds strong enough to be called storms anywhere else, cactus patches everywhere, and only the lizards finding shade. "Horse, this has got to be the last place God made, and He sure didn't make it with cowboys in mind. It just don't get no worse than this, I suspect." He said it to himself as much as for the benefit of a chestnut gelding between his legs.

Against the distant horizon, Billy could see rolling hills, not quite tall enough to be called mountains, but with enough elevation to create plenty of canyons and arroyos where a group of men could set up a camp that would be hard to find and easy to defend.

Billy removed his hat and sleeved sweat off his forehead, blinking as the alkali burned his eyes and made his nose sting. He was beginning to feel uneasy.

The tracks led off to the northwest now, making a turn he hadn't expected.

A few red oak trees, mesquite bushes, and scrawny live oak began to appear as the ground rose and the air became cooler at the higher altitudes. Billy was relieved. He had been concerned about the lack of cover on the desertlike plains of the past ten miles. It would had been a dangerous place to be if he had come across any of Cherokee Bill's bunch.

Just before dusk, when the light was failing and the sun was near the western horizon, he saw the cattle tracks leading into a canyon. "Looks like we might have found the bastards' hideout, Horse,'' he said under his breath. Billy pulled his animals to a halt and sat there, surveying the surrounding hills. After studying things for a time, he reined off to the west and made his way up the side of a steep hill, staying in the heaviest cover he could find, walking his mounts, moving as quietly as he knew how from one thicket of trees to the next. He had seen what looked like a thin column of smoke coming from the canyon, a camp fire.

When he was in sight of the rim of the canyon, he swung down to tie off his horses, pulling his Sharps rifle and chambering one round. He crept forward on the balls of his feet, pausing often to listen for a sound that didn't belong in this empty wilderness.

And then he heard it, the mournful bawl of a cow or a steer coming from the canyon floor. Cows made a habit of calling out to each other before they bedded down for the night, a noise any cowboy recognized when a herd was settling.

''Paydirt,'' Billy whispered, inching forward, keeping low so as not to skyline himself when he came to the canyon rim.

He found what he expected when he had a view of the winding canyon below. Scattered across a half mile of grass on either side of a slender creek, small groups of longhorns grazed. Some had already picked out a spot to lie down until dawn—or until something spooked them.

A crude cabin fashioned out of logs sat near the creek, and smoke was curling from a stone-and-mud chimney. In a pole corral behind the cabin, he counted nine horses. For the moment, no one was about—no one he could see.

They'll have guards posted, he told himself. They won't be crazy enough to think they're plumb safe.

He swept the mouth of the canyon with a lingering gaze, to find any sign that someone was keeping an eye out for uninvited visitors. Billy was certain he'd found the outlaws' camp. This wasn't cow country and the beeves were being held together, most likely until a running iron could be used to change brands.

"This ain't gonna be easy." Counting the horses he could see gave him an indication of the number of men keeping watch over the cattle, with maybe a spare mount or two. He'd found what he was looking for, only now he needed a way to earn the money Mr. Burnet was paying him. Getting these cows back to the Burnet Ranch promised to be a man-sized job, one he'd undertaken without giving it much serious consideration. Until now.

Dark settled over the prairies and the canyon. All along Billy had known what he would try to do if circumstances, and luck, were on his side. One thing he understood, a factor in his favor. He knew the spooky nature of longhorns about as well as any cowhand. If something frightened them, especially at night, they would scatter like leaves in the wind, a distraction that would give Billy an advantage. If things went just right. It would require a bit of careful planning on his part.

He watched more longhorns bed down and yet he still found no sign of any of the cow thieves. Some of them, perhaps most, were inside the cabin, judging by the smoke coming from the rock chimney.

Billy settled down on his haunches to wait. The shape of the canyon was just about right for a stampede to work. He was an old hand when it came to runaway longhorns, knowing full well how dangerous their horns could be when the creatures were at top speed. Plenty of green cowboys had given up their lives before they learned the lesson, but on the other side of things Cherokee Bill's men would be seasoned, experienced. Billy would have to count on Lady Luck in order for his idea to work.

SIXTEEN

A night chill came to the hills and canyons. Billy watched the outlaws' hideout, shivering inside his thin mackinaw, with the Sharps resting on his lap. It seemed odd when no one went into or came out of the cabin, and as far as he could tell no guards were posted near the canyon mouth.

He supposed it was possible that Cherokee Bill and part of his gang were elsewhere, perhaps raiding other ranches below the Red, making it a perfect time to get Mr. Burnet's cattle back if he could figure a way to get them stampeding out of the canyon in the dark. Of course, the longhorns would scatter all over creation and he'd be faced with the chore of rounding them up to get them started back south, a helluva job for one cowboy who also had to be on the lookout for cow thieves who wanted their stolen livestock back. There appeared to be no way to get it done without bloodshed and he supposed he'd known it from the beginning. But was he really up to the task? Sitting alone on a dark ridge above a hideout for an infamous rustler and killer like Cherokee Bill, most likely backed by as many as a dozen more hardcases, he began to experience serious doubts. He'd ridden off on this risky affair full of confidence. After all, he'd killed Leon Pickett easily enough, although not without a scare or two. The others he tangled with at the Burnet Ranch hadn't been much shakes with a gun—not like Pickett—and Ozark Jack was mostly bluff. But what he hoped to do here single-handed had begun to seem like a fool's move, unless he could find a way to take most of the risk out of it.

His only clear choice was the most dangerous—slip down to the floor of the canyon on foot and start shooting, making as much noise as he could with the Greener shotgun. The cattle would run, but he would be exposed, his position pinpointed for whoever was in the cabin. They'd come after him, unless he was slick enough to get back to his horses before the manhunt commenced.

"Sure wish I had just one good man to side with me," he said in a whisper. Old Juan wouldn't have been any help and Lincoln and Luis were simple cowhands, unlikely to know the first thing about guns or ducking flying lead. "I reckon it's up to me," he added softly, shivering again. "I damn sure hope I live through this so I can spend Mr. Burnet's generous wages."

He got up quietly and crept away from the rimrock with his mind made up to try a stampede by setting off the longhorns with his shotgun. Otherwise, he could wind up sitting there all night trying to think of easier ways to get the job done.

There would be a running gun battle in the dark right after the cows went on the prod. Depending on how many men were after him, and how close they got to him, he'd be relying on having a good horse under him and one hell of a lot of luck.

He approached his tethered horses carefully, making sure no one had spotted them before he had loaded all his guns—an extra pair of Colt pistols and his Winchester.

Then he rode to the west end of the canyon to begin climbing down with his Greener, his coat pockets stuffed with 10-gauge shells. He had it figured he'd be lucky to get off more than a dozen shots with the booming Greener before the cabin emptied with men out to hunt him down. But if longhorns were true to their skittish nature, the outlaws would be dodging runaway beeves with five- or six-foot horn spreads, animals that would gore a man standing in the way if the cows were frightened.

Billy mounted his chestnut and began riding a slow circle around the canyon, keeping to low ground, making as little noise as he could. He could feel his heart racing. Once events started happening, there would be precious little time to think things through. Everything would depend on what the cattle did, and how many good gunmen were inside the cabin. Once the longhorns hit open rangeland, they would run until they were exhausted or until someone turned them in a circle. Billy doubted he'd have time or opportunity to get the lead cows turned—he'd be too busy dodging bullets. But if his idea worked and he could drop a few rustlers from their saddles, it would serve to discourage them, hopefully long enough for Billy to get as many of the cows as he could headed south for the Red River. When the longhorns ran out of the canyon, he needed to be there, if he could, requiring a fast climb back to his horses and a speedy trip around the back side of the canyon where he was riding now, if he was to stand any chance of getting the cattle headed in the right direction. All this with Cherokee Bill's men out to kill him—they'd come boiling out of the canyon as soon as they could get horses saddled. It was one hell of an ambitious plan, and things had to work just right if he meant to get back to the ranch without bullet holes in his hide.

His doubts continued to grow as he rode quietly through the dark to find a place to tie his horses.

• • •

An owl hooted somewhere in trees dotting the canyon floor. He made his way down a steep rock embankment with the Greener balanced in one hand. In spite of an early spring chill, he was sweating. In moments the silence around him would end abruptly, and from then on a wrong move could end his life or leave him seriously wounded. The same shotgun he carried now had cut two of Cherokee Bill's men to ribbons, and for some reason the memory of those killings returned. The rustlers who got away surely came back here to warn Cherokee Bill, and to give him the name of the man who killed French and his partner. It seemed odd that an outlaw with Cherokee Bill's deadly reputation had no night guards posted around his hideout—there was no mistaking the trail of the herd Billy followed here. The longhorns bedded in this canyon belonged to Burnet. So why wasn't someone keeping an eye on them?

He reached the bottom of the cliff and made his way through a red oak thicket, until he could see the dark shapes of resting cattle spread the length of the canyon floor. This was about as close as he dared get, seeing as these cows were of the longhorn variety. A longhorn possessed many of the cautious habits of a truly wild animal, like deer, and when any unusual noise or movement occurred, they would rise to their feet and take off in a headlong run.

No sense wasting any more time, he decided, jacking back the hammers on his Greener. Rocky cliffs on three sides would make the roar of his scattergun seem that much louder.

He fired both barrels into the air, flinching when the noise hurt his ears, and began reloading both tubes before the clap of exploding gunpowder died down.

And true to their nature, longhorns all over the canyon came lunging to their feet, tails in the air, snorting. He fired both barrels again. Even with his ears ringing, he could hear the all too familiar rumble of cattle hooves moving at a run just as the sound made by twin 10-gauge shells began to fade.

He loaded and fired twice more, watching swirling groups of terrified longhorns break into a charge toward the canyon mouth.

"That oughta do it," he said, wheeling to scramble back up the rock face to his horses.

He'd just made a choice, a dangerous one, and a voice inside his head, his father's voice, kept saying over and over again, "Billy boy, you gotta be one of the craziest kids a man ever tried to raise! You ain't got a lick o' sense!"

Galloping cattle were still streaming out of the canyon by the time he got to the entrance. Bawling, charging longhorns raced blindly behind the leaders, bellowing, hooking their sharp horns in wide, sweeping motions at anything and everything in their path. And it was quickly evident plenty of other ranchers had been losing cattle to these thieves, since the number of cows stampeding out of the canyon exceeded anything Mr. Burnet had said he'd lost. Close to a hundred head of rampaging longhorns came in a rush of hooves and horns between rocky cliffs, spotted cows and brindle mixes with a few solid whites and dark browns bunched together. And because of their number, Billy saw opportunity at his doorstep. If he hid his horses in trees near the entrance, he would have a perfect firing position when members of the gang got saddled and came after the beeves.

He reined over into a stand of cedar and oak and jumped from the saddle with his Winchester, levering a round into the chamber as he hurried to find cover within range of the canyon mouth. He found a pile of rocks fallen from the canyon rim and settled down out of sight to wait for horsemen.

The last longhorns came bounding out of the canyon, bellowing in a strange cattle chorus, chasing after the leaders. And for a moment or two, when the cows ran off onto the inky prairie, things were quiet.

Half a minute later, two horses galloped from the opening with riders on their backs. Billy had raised his rifle to his shoulder for a pair of easy shots, when something about the two men made him hesitate—they were too small to be men. One was clinging to his horse's back like a tick on a bloodhound, while the other was scarcely larger.

"Hold it there!" Billy cried, keeping his rifle sights on the pair. "Jerk those horses down, boys, or I'll empty your saddles!"

Both riders reined their horses to a sliding stop only a few yards from the rocks where Billy was hiding.

"Don't shoot!" a thin voice shouted.

The other rider raised both hands in the air. "Don't shoot us, mister," he said. "We was only chasin' after them cows what run off."

"Who are you!" Billy demanded, judging both boys to be less than fifteen or sixteen.

"I'm Tommy," one said. "Tommy Lee Woods. I work fer Bill lookin' after his cows."

"They ain't his cows!" Billy snapped. "Some of 'em that run past me was wearing the 6666 brand."

A silence followed while one youth looked at the other. "I know what you's talkin' about, mister, only we ain't got nothin' to do with no brandin'."

"Where's Cherokee Bill?" Billy asked.

Again there was a silence.

"Him an' the others headed down to Texas. Somebody shot two of Bill's cowboys an' he said he wasn't gonna take nobody shootin' down none of his men. They took plenty of guns with 'em an' Bill said they'd be back real soon."

"When did they leave?" Billy wanted to know, lowering his Winchester. These kids were harmless.

"Yesterday. Real early. Are you a lawman, mister? Can't see no badge on account of it's so dark."

"I'm not the law. I work for the 6666 brand. I came after the cattle Cherokee Bill stole from us an' I intend to take 'em back to Texas with me."

"You're liable to run right into Bill hisself," the other boy stammered.

"Suits the hell outta me. Now I'm gonna climb on my horse an' the two of your are gonna help me get those longhorns headed south. Either one of you tries to run off, I'll put a hole in you."

"Yessir," both boys said in unison.

Billy turned for his chestnut. By a twist of fate he'd come to Cherokee Bill's hideout at just the right time to avoid a big gunfight, and now he had a couple of helpers to get Mr. Burnet's cows headed in the right direction.

But suddenly, as he stepped into the saddle, a chilling thought entered his brain. Cherokee Bill and his men were headed for the ranch looking to even a score—with him.

SEVENTEEN

Small bunches of cattle here hidden in almost every dark thicket. Many were still agitated by the gunshots, milling here and there, snorting at a horse and rider when Billy or one of the kids attempted to push them out on open ground to form a herd. It would be hours before some of the wild critters settled down enough to drive them, but as the group of longhorns grew larger, he was satisfied. Come daylight, when he could see the brands on their hides, he'd make a count of Burnet cattle. He would turn the rest over to the closest peace officer—if he could find one in this empty country.

The boy named Tommy rode over, his sorrel horse covered with lather. ''That's nearly all we can find, mister,'' he said, still sounding fearful.

Billy decided to take it easy on the kids, even though they were in the employ of a cow thief. ''Stay with me an' help me keep 'em together till daylight. Then you an' your little pard are free to go. But I'm gonna give you a little advice, son. I wouldn't stay on with Cherokee Bill's outfit, don't matter how badly you need a job. You're liable to get killed over day wages when the law comes after Bill, maybe spend some time in jail if you're lucky.''

''We been talkin' about it. Only Bill said he'd kill us if we cut out on him.''

''It's up to you,'' Billy replied casually, edging his horse closer to a pair of cows hanging back at the rear of the herd. ''I'm only givin' you fair warning. When I get to the closest U.S. marshal, I'm gonna report what I found in that canyon back yonder. You can bet your young ass the law will show up 'fore too long.''

''But we didn't steal no cows, mister. All we git paid to do is see after 'em, make sure they don't wander out of this canyon till somebody changes them brands so Bill can drive 'em up to Dodge City or Newton.''

''You'd still have to explain it to a judge an' make him believe you.''

Tommy appeared to shrink in the saddle. ''Times have been real hard lately, mister. Me an' Charlie sure do need this here job.''

Billy had an idea. ''Tell you what, son. I ain't really got the authority to offer you no wages from the Burnet spread, but I figure Miz Burnet would be glad to pay you decent if you helped me drive this herd back to the ranch.''

Tommy gazed at the dark horizon in front of them for a moment. ''We's sure as heck liable to run into Bill an' the rest of 'em, 'cause that 6666 ranch is where they was headed. Said they was gonna kill some gunfighter calls hisself Billy Blue. He's the feller that shot French an' McWilliams, accordin' to Ozark Jack an' Lefty.''

Billy felt a little knot form in his belly. ''They rode all that way to kill one man?'' he asked. He wondered if the outlaws would take out their vengeance against anyone they found at the ranch. But he was powerless to warn Miz Burnet and the others in time.

Tommy nodded. ''Bill said he was gonna make an example out of whoever this Blue feller is, so folks won't be takin' no potshots at his boys no more. Ozark Jack acted a little nervous about it, 'cause somebody tol' him Billy Blue was the gent who out-drawed Leon Pickett in a fair fight down at Fort Worth. It was Ozark Jack who was against the idea; only Bill said he wasn't scared of nobody."

The boy named Charlie rode over, pushing four cows into the herd. "That's near 'bout the last of 'em," he said.

Tommy leaned out of his saddle to speak to Charlie. "This here feller has offered us wages to help drive these cows back to Texas. I tol' him we sure needed a job."

"I ain't all that fond of the one we got," Charlie said as he thought about it. "Cherokee Bill ain't the easiest feller to git along with."

Tommy turned back to Billy. "It's settled then, mister. We ride with you an' these longhorns back to Texas. You can pay us whatever you figure it's worth."

"Can't say for sure," Billy told him, "but knowin' the boss lady an' Mr. Burnet like I think I do, it'll be fair wages."

Tommy and Charlie nodded. It was Charlie who spoke next.

"You mind tellin' us your name, mister? That way, we'll know how you're supposed to be called."

"Name's Billy Blue," he said.

Tommy's jaw fell open. "You're the feller Cherokee Bill rode to Texas to kill. You're the gunslick who shot down none other than Leon Pickett that time."

Billy waited a moment, thinking. "It's true. I killed Leon Pickett an' two of Cherokee Bill's rustlers. Woulda killed a few more if they hadn't tucked tail an' run off so quick. I never thought of me bein' a gunslick. I just did what I had to do when Pickett came after me. It started over a woman."

"You outgunned him in a fair fight?"

"I'd call it fair. I gave him the first pull an' he took it."

"Holy cow!" Charlie exclaimed. "Leon Pickett was near 'bout the meanest man with a gun who ever walked the earth, accordin' to Cherokee Bill. Bill said he wasn't scared to draw against nobody, 'cept maybe Leon Pickett an' ol' Tom Spoon. Tom Spoon's in prison now, an' somebody told Bill that Pickett got shot down in Texas. You must be awful fast with that gun you're carryin' on your hip."

"Faster'n some, maybe. I don't make no regular habit of testin' myself in that line of work."

"Bill said he was gonna kill you, one way or another, fer what you done to French an' McWilliams," Tommy said.

Billy took a glance at the night sky overhead. "He may get it done. Time'll tell, I reckon."

"You sure don't sound all that worried about it, Mr. Blue."

"No sense worryin' 'bout things till there's a need. Right now all I'm worried about is getting these cattle across the Red an' back to the Burnet Ranch. If Cherokee Bill an' some of his shootists get in my way, then I figure we'll get a chance to find out who's faster—and who's got the best aim."

"I've seen Bill shoot men," Tommy said. "He's faster'n a greased pig with a six-shooter."

Billy shrugged as the longhorns lined out in good trail fashion, plodding south toward the river. "Maybe he is fast. If he tries to take these stolen cows back, I suppose we'll see if he's faster'n me." A thought occurred to Billy. "How many men has he got with him?"

"Six, besides him," Charlie replied. "An' ain't a one of 'em scared to use a gun."

What Charlie described were long odds. But Billy wouldn't let that fact keep him from trying to earn his money. What lay in the back of his mind was the safety of

Mrs. Burnet and Melissa if Cherokee Bill attacked the ranch. Juan and Lincoln and Luis wouldn't be able to put up much of a fight.

Billy felt sure he knew what Mr. Burnet would want him to do in a situation like this—save his family. But how could he get these cows back to the ranch in time to be of any help?

One choice, a poor risk, might be the answer. If he trusted Tommy and Charlie to push these cows down to the river and then across, he could put his chestnut into a hard run, changing to the bay as soon as the chestnut was winded, gaining as much ground on Cherokee Bill as he could by keeping a fresh horse underneath him. It would be putting a hell of a lot of faith in two young boys who worked for an outlaw. He decided the best way to convince them to stay honest was to run as much bluff on them as he could, seeing as how they knew his name, and about how he shot down Pickett.

He turned to Charlie and Tommy while they rode at the back of the quieting herd. "Tell you what I'm gonna do, boys," he began, putting as much edge in his voice as he knew how. "It'd crossed my mind to just up an' kill the both of you once we got across the Red. Be the easiest way for me—"

"Please don't shoot us, Mr. Blue!" Tommy exclaimed. "You done offered us wages to help with these here cows. How come you to change your mind on it?"

"We ain't got a gun betwixt us," Charlie added in a fearful voice, showing both hands to be empty. "Me an' Tommy ain't never stole a cow in our whole lives! Honest!"

Billy wagged his head like he wasn't convinced. "I gotta get back to the ranch an' help Mr. Burnet's womenfolk. There ain't but a couple of range cowboys an' this old Mexican to keep Cherokee Bill from harmin' those women.

If I kill the two of you, I can let these longhorns wander while I ride hard for the ranch. Maybe I can make it in time.''

Charlie's lips were trembling. ''We'd give you our word by all that's holy we'd take this herd plumb to California if you told us where to take 'em. Ain't that right, Tommy?''

''Right as rain,'' Tommy promised. ''We ain't rustlers, like we already told you, Mr. Blue. Ain't neither one of us got no family hereabouts an' we took this job 'cause it's all we could find when we rode west from Fort Smith. We'd take this herd to the 6666 Ranch straight as an arrow flies. That way, you can ride hard to help them women—''

''How do I know I can trust you?'' Billy asked.

''About all we've got is the clothes we's wearin' an' our word that we'd do just like you say. A man's word is sometimes all he's got.''

Billy gave them the appearance of thinking it over. ''If I did trust you, an' you double-cross me, I'll come lookin' for you an' I damn sure wouldn't give you no second chances. I'd kill you deader'n fenceposts when I caught up to you.'' He found it hard to hand out this warning with a straight face, seeing how scared the kids were of him.

''You ain't got a thing to worry 'bout, Mr. Blue,'' Charlie told him. ''Just tell us how to find that ranch over in Texas an' we'll be there with these cows, come hell or high water.''

''Charlie's tellin' you honest, Mr. Blue,'' Tommy chimed in. ''We'd be there, wherever that ranch is at. But if I was you, I'd ride real careful in case you run across Bill an' them boys he's got. They's killers, every last one of 'em.''

''That part don't worry me,'' Billy said. ''It's bein' sure you boys won't double-cross me that has me thinkin' things over real hard.''

"I'll swear to it," Tommy said. "I'll swear we'll deliver these cows, no matter what."

"Me too," Charlie added. "We'd have to be plumb loco to even think 'bout double-crossin' the man who shot Leon Pickett. Why, even Cherokee Bill said Pickett was one of the best gunmen who ever strapped on a six-shooter."

Billy's mind was made up. "I'll leave you some food, a bit of jerky an' some biscuits. Ride due south to the river an' cross over where there's two big willow trees standin' right together. No quicksand there. Then swing southwest. Look for a big caprock mountain maybe fifty miles below the river. You'll see it for a couple of days before you get to it. Ride around to the south of that mesa an' you'll be on 6666 range. But you damn sure better show up. Understood?"

"Yessir," Tommy said. "Only what're we supposed to do if we run into Bill? He'll kill us sure if he thinks we stole these cows ourselves, or if we was aimin' to take 'em back to where Bill stole 'em in the first place."

Billy swept the dark horizon again, judging it was getting close to midnight. "You leave Cherokee Bill an' his friends to me. Just make damn sure these longhorns get to the Burnet Ranch inside of five days."

"You ain't got a worry in the world when it comes to that," Tommy said.

He took a bundle of jerky from one of the packs, and a sack of Miz Burnet's biscuits, handing them over to Charlie. "Don't forget what I said. Cross the river where them two big willows hang over the water. Then angle southwest till you spot that flat mountain."

"We'll be there, Mr. Blue," Charlie promised, taking a strip of jerky for himself. "Sure glad you decided to trust us. We ain't lookin' to fill no grave."

Billy decided to add one last bit of bluff to the message he gave them. "Fillin' a grave is exactly what you'll be doin' if these cattle don't show up at the 6666. Five days is what you've got.''

''We'll push 'em as hard as they'll drive,'' Tommy said, with a mouthful of jerky bulging in his cheek.

Billy reined his chestnut to ride wide of the herd, pulling the bay by its leadrope. He heeled his mount to a trot, so as not to spook the cattle any more than necessary.

As he rode off, he grinned a little, believing he'd put just enough scare into Tommy and Charlie to convince them he meant what he said. It was easy to see they believed him. It was odd how a man's reputation could sometimes accomplish more than anything he actually did himself. Killing Leon Pickett had turned out to be more than winning a duel with pistols. Even a badman the likes of Cherokee Bill had evidenced fear of Pickett. Billy wondered how events might have turned out if he'd know all about Pickett's mean reputation beforehand—before he killed him. It might have put a little too much edge on his nerves that day.

EIGHTEEN

The chestnut's long strides covered ground at a lope with the same ease the shorter-coupled bay galloped without the weight of a rider. As sunrise pinked eastern skies to his left, Billy caught sight of the wandering course of the Red River in the distance.

He'd forgotten about the cattle for now, intent upon making the Burnet Ranch as quickly as he could. Charlie and Tommy were unlikely to betray him with the threats Billy made still ringing in their ears. But the real trouble lay ahead, at the ranch, if Cherokee Bill and his bunch meant to do the Burnet family harm over something he'd done. The responsibility weighed heavily on his mind as miles passed beneath the chestnut's flying hooves.

As he neared the river, he saw the glimmer of a camp fire on the south bank, the Texas side of the boundary into Indian Territory. Caution forced Billy to swing wide of open country to ride through post oak and cedar, until he made sure who was at the fire. Cherokee Bill and his gang might be camped there, or it might only be the campsite of a traveler. A careful man who wanted to stay alive in hostile land made sure of his surroundings before he rode out in plain sight.

When he was less than a quarter mile from the river, in dawn's early light, he could make out a lone figure with a horse ground-hitched near the flames.

"Looks safe enough," he mumbled, aiming for the river, where he could cross without quicksand bogs east of the willows he'd told Charlie and Tommy about.

As soon as he rode into view from the fire across the river, the lone cowboy stood up, cradling a rifle. Billy waved and sent his chestnut into the murky, shallow waters while he led his bay packhorse.

On the southern bank he swung toward the fire, watching a man with a handlebar mustache wearing two ivory-handled pistols at his waist and keeping a close eye on Billy as he approached.

"Howdy," Billy shouted from a distance. "No need for that rifle. I'm passin' through to the Burnet spread."

"That'll be Burke Burnet," a deep voice replied, and the end of his rifle lowered. "Ride up an' have a cup of coffee, so long as you've got peaceful intentions. How is it you're headed down to Burke's place?"

Billy rode to the fire and halted his horses. "I work for Mr. Burnet. I'm new to the job. He hired me to keep an eye on things at the ranch while he headed up to Kansas Territory with a herd of steers."

"Swing down. I'm Heck Thomas, United States deputy marshal for the Western District. You're welcome to what I've got in the way of vittles."

Billy almost couldn't believe his ears. He swung his right leg over the cantle and stepped to the ground—if there was one thing he needed in the midst of all this cow stealing, it was a U.S. marshal. "Sure glad to know who you are," Billy said as he came into camp with his handshake extended. "I'm Billy Blue, and I've followed a stolen herd of Mr. Burnet's cows all the way into the Nations. Feller by the name of Cherokee Bill had 'em hid in a box canyon—''

Thomas interrupted him. ''I know that name. Billy Blue is who I'm talkin' about. Hell, every lawman in these parts knows about Cherokee Bill. But you're the man who shot it out with Leon Pickett.'' He looked Billy up and down before he took his hand. ''I expected you to be a mite older.''

They shook. Billy wasn't quite sure what to say. ''Don't know as age had anything to do with it. Pickett called me out. I let him have the first pull. He was slow, I reckon. Slower'n me, anyhow.''

Thomas frowned. ''Pickett wasn't slow. You must be pretty fast with that shootin' iron. Or could be you was just lucky. Caught Leon when he was drunk, maybe.''

''Never thought about it much, really,'' he lied. ''He was the first man I ever had to shoot in a contest at the draw. I was a fraction quicker.''

''I heard about it,'' Thomas replied. ''Now, pour yourself a cup of coffee an' tell me about this business with Cherokee Bill an' stolen cows. We've been lookin' for Bill for a sizable number of years now. He's a hard bastard to find.''

Billy walked to the fire, taking a tin cup from an open pack resting near a circle of firestones. ''I didn't find him, but I found the cows he stole from Burke Burnet. I expected to have my hands full of trouble gettin' 'em back, only I found a couple of kids watchin' over the herd. Bill an' six more of his bunch are headed down to Mr. Burnet's place to square things with me, an' it's all because I shot a couple of his boys who were runnin' a hot iron over some 6666 ranch stock, changin' brands. One was named French. The other was some guy called McWilliams. Then I had a run-in with a couple more of Cherokee Bill's boys, one bein' Ozark Jack Berlin. Didn't none of 'em strike me as bein' all that tough, only I hear Cherokee Bill is hard, like nails. I'm not countin' on him bein' so easy to handle."

Thomas was giving Billy a curious stare. "You sound like a man who's a helluva lot older, a man with considerable experience with a gun. Unless my eyes have gone bad on me, you don't look old enough to know your way round a gun all that well."

Billy poured a cupful of dark liquid that reminded him of blackstrap syrup, although it smelled like coffee—burnt coffee left too long near the flames. He was relieved to have run across a peace officer in a spot where he never expected to find one. He blew steam away from the rim of his cup. "If you ain't got more pressin' business, I could use a hand down at the Burnet Ranch. There's women there—Mr. Burnet's wife an' his daughter—an' only an old Mexican and a couple of range cowboys to protect 'em if Cherokee Bill shows up. The kids who was watchin' the herd at Bill's hideout are drivin' the cattle back this way, to the river. But if I was Mr. Burke Burnet, I'd be a lot more worried 'bout my womenfolk that I would be a herd of longhorns."

"Understandable," Thomas said, tossing out the last of his coffee. "I'll saddle my horse an' we'll head down that way. Only I think maybe you've made a mistake."

"What mistake is that?" Billy asked.

"Trustin' a couple of kids who rode for Bill. They's liable to drive those cows most anyplace—except back to a ranch where they got stole in the first place.'

"I could be wrong," Billy agreed, remembering his conversation with Tommy and Charlie. "But Mr. Burnet can raise more cows if he loses this bunch, but he sure can't raise no more daughters as pretty as Melissa, nor no finer woman than Mrs. Burnet."

"Seems you're a bit taken with his daughter, Mr. Blue, if I didn't mistake that tone in your voice."

Billy knew he was blushing. "I wouldn't say I was taken with her, Marshal. Only, she's a mighty pretty gal, when she ain't mad."

Thomas grunted, heading over to his saddle and gear near the firepit. "All women get mad once in a while, son. It's like wet weather. You gotta have some every now an' then."

Marshal Thomas was a stocky sort, yet he rode a horse with all the ease of a slender man. He carried two Colt Peacemakers and wore polished stovepipe boots. A Winchester .44 was booted to his saddle. He rode an odd-colored buttermilk roan gelding with a ewe neck and high withers, but the horse could cover ground at a long lope and it showed some thoroughbred breeding. Thomas seemed to know the country they were in, heading for the Burnet Ranch like he'd been that direction dozens of times.

Billy noticed the marshal had callused hands and a hard look in general, the way a man appears when he's been in plenty of tight spots and come out on top.

"You ever come face-to-face with Cherokee Bill?" Thomas asked as their horses crested a brush-covered knob at mid-morning.

"Never have," Billy replied. "A feller told me he ain't no Cherokee Indian at all . . . that he's a black man."

"You got good information, Billy. He took up with a handful of Cherokee renegades after he was wanted by the law over in Arkansas, Judge Parker's court. The judge had him set for a hangin'."

Billy remembered what little he'd been told about the black outlaw. "He feels safe in the Nations because there ain't much law, to speak of."

"It's a helluva big place," Thomas said. "The army does what it can, an' we've got a couple dozen deputy marshals who patrol some of it. But a man who knows the land can hide damn near forever up yonder . . . unless he leaves a trail a blind man can follow. Bill's smart. We thought we had him a time or two, but he got away clean as a whistle."

"He feels mighty brave when it comes to raidin' Mr. Burnet's herds. I reckon he knows when most of the ranch hands are off with Mr. Burnet, trailin' steers up to Kansas."

"I sure as hell hope we run into him."

"Those kids swore he was headed this way to get revenge for what I done to French an' McWilliams. I just hope we ain't too late to keep him an' his men from doin' any harm to the women at the ranch."

Thomas glanced down at the foamy lather collecting on the neck and shoulders of his roan. "We're pushin' our horses 'bout as hard as we can. Fact is, we're gonna have to let 'em blow in a mile or two. Ain't no horse can run all day like this. They'd be road-foundered."

Billy nodded, for he understood. "I've got this spare bay, an' if you've got no objections I'll change horses an' keep on ridin' hard ahead of you. Maybe if I can get to the ranch first, I can distract 'em long enough for you to catch up."

Thomas gave him a quizzical look. "I ain't got you figured yet, Billy Blue—if you're as tough as you say, or if you're just plain crazy an' lucky."

The way Thomas said it carried no intended offense. "Maybe a little of both," Billy replied, grinning. "Maybe I was just lucky when I got Leon Pickett an' them other two, but my pappy used to say he'd rather be lucky than good any ol' time."

Thomas chuckled, then his expression turned serious. "Most men I've known make their own luck, both the good an' the bad. It kinda depends."

"I'm inclined to agree," Billy told him, "only there's times when it helps to have Lady Luck on your side."

"She's a fickle bitch," Thomas said, sighting along the

tops of hills in front of them. "Sometimes a man can't hardly lose at nothin' he tries. Then, real sudden-like, everything goes haywire for no damn reason at all."

Billy felt his chestnut's strides begin to falter some. He turned to Thomas. "I'll change horses on the fly an' push for the ranch as hard as I can, Marshal. Been thinkin' about those women, an' what would happen if Cherokee Bill makes up his mind to attack the ranch house."

"I imagine you've been thinkin' about one of them women in particular," Thomas said.

The marshal pointed southwest. "Make that change to your bay an' get there quick as you can. I won't be very damn far behind you."

Billy pulled the bay alongside his chestnut, kicking his feet out of the stirrups to make a jump for the bay's back while both horses were galloping. Swinging his left leg over the cantle so he rode sidesaddle for a moment, he made the leap with little effort and landed on the bay's back.

"You made that look easy," Thomas said. "If you're as good with a gun as you are with horses, you'll keep Bill occupied till I can get to the ranch."

Billy accepted the compliment with a grin. "A horse don't shoot back, but don't you worry none. I'll give Mr. Cherokee Bill all the trouble he can handle—if I ain't already too late."

He rode off at a harder run, leading his chestnut, hearing the drum of shod hooves over hardpan as he left Marshal Thomas far behind. His thoughts drifted to Melissa, then Mrs. Burnet and the Indian girl, Pia, wondering what a gang of outlaws would do to all three women if Juan and Luis and Lincoln couldn't stand off a pack of experienced shooters. Billy felt sure Miz Burnet could shoot, adding to the bullets thrown at Bill's gang if they rushed the main house.

Melissa probably didn't know which end of a gun fired lead.

The sun was a red ball hovering above the horizon when he thought he heard the distant crackle of gunshots. He was still several miles from the ranch, making a circle around the side of the mesa that would take him to ranch headquarters. He was on Burnet land now—he'd been expecting trouble ever since he rode past a boundary stake hours earlier.

He heard the noises again, and they were far too close to be coming from the ranch. Billy could only guess what was happening. Cherokee Bill had run across Lincoln and Luis riding herd, catching them away from the protection of ranch buildings. Billy knew neither cowboy stood much of a chance of putting up a fight against outlaws and gunmen who knew their trade.

NINETEEN

He found Luis Maldonado's body first, lying facedown in a dry arroyo surrounded by blood seeping into the sandy bed of a seasonal stream. In the dusky darkness it was hard to tell if the vaquero was still breathing. Until Billy dismounted. Off in the distance he could hear cattle stampeding into the hills.

He knelt beside Luis, listening to his ragged breathing.

"I think I know what happened," Billy said, gently pushing the Mexican over on his back. "Some rustlers showed up. Damn it, you shouldn't have tried to shoot it out with them . . ."

Luis's eyes batted open. He tried to focus on Billy's face for a moment. "Cherokee . . . Bill," he whispered. "I . . . see . . . him clear."

"I tried to get back in time," Billy told him. "I rode as hard as I could. Where is Lincoln?"

"He . . . ride . . . hard for . . . the ranch. To . . . tell Señora Burnet what . . ." His voice trailed off and pink foam bubbled from his lips. Billy could see half a dozen or more gunshot wounds all over Luis's chest. At least one bullet had torn through a lung. Men seldom outlived this kind of injury. It was usually a slow and painful death.

Billy gave the arroyo a quick glance. The vaquero's horse was nowhere in sight, and it would take time to to tie him across the chestnut's saddle to take him back to the ranch. "I'll come back for you," Billy promised, knowing how empty it sounded to a man who had suffered through so much pain, a man who was clearly dying. "I've got to make a try at savin' the womenfolk. Sure hope you can understand."

Luis nodded just once before his eyelids closed. A final breath whispered from his lips and then he lay still.

Billy ran over to the chestnut and swung aboard, a curious mix of anger and dread tightening his chest. He hoped he would not be too late to get to the ranch, before the gang made its move on ranch headquarters—an attack that was a result of what he'd done to a couple of gunmen named French and McWilliams.

He rode off at a gallop, pulling the tired bay behind him with the lead rope dallied around his saddle horn. He'd ridden less than a quarter mile before he heard gunshots again—the pop of rifles and the crackle of smaller arms.

"Damn!" he hissed, clenching his teeth. Luis, a simple Mexican cowboy, was dead as a result of his actions, and now it sounded like the Burnet Ranch was under siege.

He pulled his Winchester, making sure a cartridge was in the firing chamber and resting the barrel across the pommel of his saddle as he asked his horse for more speed. To the west, near the base of the flat mesa, the rattle of guns grew louder.

As he crossed a rocky ridge that would give him a view of the main house and the barns, his horse snorted and shied from something lying in his path. Billy drew back on the reins, and what he saw convinced him that Lincoln Jones hadn't made it to the ranch to warn the women, or Juan, about what was headed their way. Jones lay in a heap beside the crumpled carcass of his dead horse. The outlaws had shot his horse out from under him and then riddled his body with bullets.

In a shallow valley where the main house and barns stood, Billy saw the wink of muzzle flashes and heard the bang of guns.

"I'm too late," he whispered, heeling his horse into a full gallop.

Charging downslope, he very nearly ran headlong into a man on a horse driving a small bunch of cattle away from the ranch. In the dark he couldn't see the cowboy clearly, although he was sure it wasn't Juan. Billy whipped his Winchester to his shoulder just as a gun banged in the rustler's hand. The sizzle of a bullet whispered above the crown of Billy's hat.

He fired when his sights were steady—as steady as they could be aboard the back of a running horse. The explosion of a .44 shell spooked his horse and it shied away from the noise, swerving left, almost tossing him from the saddle seat.

A cry of pain followed the blast from Billy's rifle and the cow thief threw his arms in the air as he tumbled off the rump of his horse. Cattle bellowed and turned in every direction to escape the banging guns.

Billy check-reined his chestnut back toward the ranch buildings, while levering another cartridge into the firing chamber of his rifle. "That's one less son of a bitch I gotta worry about," he muttered, tossing the leadrope on his bay to one side so his chestnut could lengthen its strides.

The dark outlines of the house, bunkhouse, and barns made dim silhouettes against a night sky as he rode at full gallop toward the ranch. Now and then a muzzle flash blossomed from a window of the house, proof that someone was still alive inside, firing back at the gang.

Less than a quarter mile from the ranch he glimpsed two

riders driving cows and calves out of a corral behind one of the loafing sheds. As best he could, Billy took aim and fired three rapid shots.

Both outlaws halted their horses momentarily, firing pistols in Billy's direction, then one spurred his horse out of the corral and took off for the hills. The second gunman took flight after his partner, bending low in the saddle as if he, too, wanted no more of this fight.

Leaves four, Billy thought, doubting that either of the two runaways would be Cherokee Bill. The leader of the gang wouldn't tuck tail and run—men with tall reputations had to be convinced with some lead persuasion.

A rifle cracked from a window of the bunkhouse and one more outlaw was dumped from his saddle. Another member of the gang swung his horse toward Billy, for the moment ignoring gunfire being returned from the ranch buildings. The chestnut's head bobbed up and down with the power of its run as the distance to the ranch closed—Billy could hear the gelding's labored breath as its hooves pounded hard ground.

A stocky outlaw wearing a flop-brim hat wheeled his horse away from one of the barns—the glint of a rifle in moonlight gave his position away before Billy saw the horse turn. The man was watching Billy.

Billy fired at the outlaw, knowing his hurried shot stood little chance of finding its target. He chambered another round just as the stocky cowboy fired back.

Billy felt the chestnut falter, stumbling, then it went down on its chest, pitching Billy over its neck. He flew through the air and landed on his chest, tasting a mouthful of dirt just as all the air was driven from his lungs.

He lay there a moment, stunned, still holding his Winchester in his right fist. The outlaw had shot his horse, one of the most cowardly things any man could do when a fight was between men.

"You bastard!" he hissed, coming to his hands and knees.

Behind him he could hear his wounded chestnut struggling, grunting, trying to regain its feet.

The heavyset outlaw came spurring toward him, galloping through a gate in a corral and circling one side of the barn. Billy jutted his jaw, bringing the rifle to his shoulder while rocking back on his haunches.

He fired too quickly, out of anger, with the sounds of his injured horse bringing his rage to a boil. The shot went wide and he knew it. The whine of spent lead was hard to hear above the rumble of stampeding cattle and galloping horses, and the occasional gunshots being fired at the ranch mingling with the bang of guns coming from ranch-house windows.

Billy chambered the last shell in the loading tube of his Winchester while the gunman charged toward him. I can't miss this time, he thought, steadying his gunsights, clamping the rifle to his shoulder.

Before his finger closed around the trigger, he heard a gun pop near the bunkhouse. The rider galloping in his direction stiffened, looking back over his shoulder just as Billy fired.

He'd missed again, but the outlaw found himself in a deadly crossfire coming from Billy and the bunkhouse. He jerked his horse to the east and rode toward a thin line of oak trees just putting forth spring leaves. In the dark, now that Billy's rifle was empty, it was too late to shoot at the escaping gunman before he made it into the forest.

"Son of a bitch!" Billy cried, scrambling to his feet. He had the strange feeling that the man who'd disappeared into the red oaks was Cherokee Bill.

Now the shooting stopped entirely. A strange quiet came over the ranch and the valley. Off somewhere in the hills beyond the ranch he could hear faint hoofbeats. At least three of the rustlers had gotten away and for the moment Billy was afoot with no way to go after them.

He knew what was expected of him first—to find out if the women at the ranch were okay. Mrs. Burnet, Melissa, and Pia were more important than chasing the survivors of this fight right at the moment, and Billy also wanted to be sure Juan had survived the gun battle.

He started walking away from his dying chestnut, preparing how he would tell Miz Burnet about Lincoln and Luis. As he strode downhill, he thumbed more cartridges into the loading gate of his rifle, just in case some of the rustlers were wounded and still dangerous at close range.

"Hello the house!" he shouted when he was in earshot. "It's me! Billy Blue!"

A lengthy silence followed, until a voice he recognized came from the bunkhouse.

"Señor Blue!"

"They're gone, Juan! Don't shoot!"

He saw a dim shape come from the bunkhouse door with a rifle, and then a woman's voice came from a window of the house.

"Is that you, Billy?"

It was Melissa's voice, and when he heard it he smiled.

"It's me. I think they've given up. I saw three men riding off to the north."

"There were eight or nine of them. Be careful. There may be more of them!"

It warmed him some to think that Melissa might care enough to be concerned for his safety. "I'm pretty sure they're all gone," he told her, nearing the front porch steps.

Mrs. Burnet came out first with a rifle in her hands. She gave the yard around the ranch house a quick inspection. "They came at us from all sides. We don't know what happened to Luis or Lincoln . . ."

Billy stopped at the porch steps, tipping his hat back with

a thumb. "I'm afraid I've got bad news, Mrs. Burnet. I found both of them on my way to the house. Luis lived long enough to tell me a little bit about what happened."

"And what about Mr. Jones?" she asked softly.

"He was dead when I found him. They'd shot his horse out from under him an' then they killed him, by the looks of things where he was layin'."

"Dear God," Mrs. Burnet sighed. "When Burke gets back, he'll be fit to be tied."

"Main thing, ma'am, is that you an' your daughter are all right."

Juan came strolling toward him from the bunkhouse as Billy added, "They was runnin' off some more of your cattle. I shot one drivin' a bunch over that hill yonder. But I don't figure your husband will care about the cows, an' it's sure a shame that Lincoln an' Luis had to lose their lives. Mr. Burnet would have wanted me to make sure you're okay."

"I suppose you're right," Mrs. Burnet said, as Melissa came out to stand beside her, wearing denim jeans and a man's work shirt. Melissa also carried a rifle, and that fact surprised Billy some.

"They'll come back, won't they?" she asked as Juan came to the porch.

"Not likely," Billy replied. "I had the good fortune to meet up with a United States marshal camped up on the Red River, an' he's headed this way. His name was Heck Thomas."

Mrs. Burnet smiled. "Why, of course, my husband knows Heck from some of our wilder days . . . when the Comanches were our worst worry."

"He should be here shortly," Billy told her. "His horse played out, or he'd be here now. Soon as he gets here and gets mounted on a fresh horse, we'll take off after Cherokee Bill an' the boys who were with him."

"I'm so sorry to hear about Lincoln and Luis," Melissa said softly. "Luis had been with us for years. And Lincoln was such a gentle man."

Billy rested his rifle against his leg. "I sure could use a cup of coffee while we wait for Marshal Thomas," he said, and then he looked at Melissa. "Wouldn't mind havin' one of them bearclaws you packed along with my jerky an' biscuits either," he added.

The young woman smiled, turning for the door. "I'll see what I can do," she said.

Juan put a hand on Billy's shoulder. "You be very lucky, señor."

"Lucky?"

"Lucky Cherokee Bill don't kill you tonight."

Billy gazed up at the stars. "Might be Cherokee Bill is the one who's lucky. I had him in my sights, only he turned just as I was pullin' the trigger. Luck was on his side, but he'd best not count on bein' so lucky the next time we meet up."

TWENTY

Melissa's smile warmed him as much as the coffee she gave him while he sat at the kitchen table waiting for Marshal Thomas to arrive, wondering why the lawman was so late getting to the ranch. Juan was in the bunkhouse with Mrs. Burnet tending to a wounded outlaw, after Billy bound the rustler's hands behind him with a length of rope. The outlaw, a half-breed Indian with a black man's darker skin and features, had refused to say a word when Billy asked him about Cherokee Bill and the others. At first Billy had wondered aloud if this rustler might be Cherokee Bill, until Juan told him otherwise—Juan had seen Cherokee Bill from a distance on a number of occasions. With a serious wound in his right side, the injured rustler might not live to see the next sunrise. It would be up to Marshal Thomas to decide what to do with him . . . if the marshal ever got there.

Billy had taken care of an unpleasant chore—shooting the chestnut horse to put it out of its misery. The rustler's bullet had shattered its shoulder, and as a man who loved horses, Billy couldn't let the animal suffer.

"We thought we'd all be killed," Melissa said, watching

him eat a bearsign, her expression serious now. "You came along just in time to save us. They were shooting at the house from every direction. There's hardly a windowpane left that isn't shot all to pieces. You got here just in time."

"Luck, I reckon. I was headed back with your stolen cattle and a couple of kids who were lookin' after 'em at the outlaws' hideout. I left the cows with those boys to get back here quick as I could, after one kid told me Cherokee Bill was aimin' for the ranch to square things for the two men I killed. I had to choose between drivin' cows or makin' sure you folks were okay. Wasn't much of a choice, really. It's what your pa would have wanted me to do. Then I ran across Marshal Heck Thomas."

She tilted her head, watching him closely. "You aren't at all like I thought you would turn out to be—an arrogant cowboy who fancies himself more than he should. You're different and I misjudged you."

Billy grinned. "No need to explain, ma'am. I never did have the best of manners around women."

"Why don't you call me Melissa."

He shrugged. "Suits me. To tell the truth I had *you* guessed wrong, Melissa. I was pretty sure you were a spoiled rich man's daughter with a bad temper. Appears I was wrong."

"I do have a bad temper sometimes." She giggled. "I get it from my father's side."

He downed the last of his coffee. "I'd better saddle a horse an' go see what's keepin' Marshal Thomas. Could be he ran right into Cherokee Bill an' his boys after they lit out of here. Not that a man like Heck Thomas can't take care of himself. And I gotta make sure those young cowboys don't double-cross me an' head the wrong direction with your daddy's cattle. It's gonna be a long night in the saddle, either way."

"Why don't you wait until morning, Billy?" she asked as he stood up.

"I'm bein' paid to do a job. Until those cows are back on Burnet land, I ain't finished. And like I said, Marshal Thomas may need a dose of help if he's tanglin' with those rustlers. I figure things will be quiet here at the ranch till I get back. Cherokee Bill won't be comin' back this way after the lickin' he took tonight."

Melissa came around the table and touched his sleeve. "Be careful, please," she said, her cheeks turning a bit pink. "I wouldn't want anything to happen to you."

Hearing the way she felt truly surprised him. "That's real nice of you, Melissa. Don't worry none. I'm pretty good at takin' care of myself."

He rode off into the night on a borrowed sorrel gelding, after stabling his bay packhorse and then saying good-bye to Mrs. Burnet and Juan, telling them what he planned to do. He was still worried over the fact that Marshal Thomas hadn't shown up, and all sorts of possibilities entered his mind. Had Cherokee Bill or one of his men gotten lucky and waylaid the marshal in the dark?

Urging the horse to a short lope, Billy rode back down the trail he'd followed to reach the ranch, remembering Melissa and some of the sweet things she said to him in the kitchen. He'd been dead wrong about her, or so it seemed. She could be as nice as any woman, when she wanted to be.

Five or six miles northeast of the ranch he reached the spot where he and Marshal Thomas had parted company. In the dark, he couldn't find any tracks, and he was left to guesswork as to what had come of the lawman, why they hadn't crossed trails. There was a chance Marshal Thomas had seen Cherokee Bill making his escape and taken off after him. On the other side of things it was possible the marshal had been ambushed. His roan gelding had been all but played out, so even if he took up the trail of the outlaws, he couldn't travel far without resting his mount. Billy continued to wonder about things as he headed for the crossing at the Red, knowing he wouldn't make it until long after daylight, perhaps the middle of the morning.

Another dark thought started to worry him. The two kids he left in charge of the herd might meet up with Cherokee Bill and double back toward the canyon with the cattle. Then he'd be in the same fix he was in when he started—having to get the cows back—only this time he'd be facing Cherokee Bill and his gang when they were ready for him, even though their number had been cut almost in half, by Billy's count.

The sorrel was rough-gaited but long on stamina, and despite a jolting ride, he was making good time.

"My ass will be sore tomorrow," he said to the gelding, as if the horse could understand.

He made the river on an exhausted animal shortly before noon, and still there had been no sign of the marshal. Now he was genuinely worried that Thomas had been bushwhacked in the dark by one of the rustlers—he and the lawman should have crossed trails long before sunrise, unless they'd simply missed each other in the darkness.

At the crossing, he couldn't find any recent horse tracks headed north.

"Bill an' his boys must've crossed someplace else," he said to himself, allowing the sorrel to drink its fill from the river before he pushed on. And on the prairie north of the river there was no sign of the stolen herd—no dust curling into the air from so many cloven hooves, no dark spots on the horizon that might be a herd of longhorns.

It was beginning to look like he'd made a bad guess about the two kids, trusting them to bring the herd south.

His threat didn't appear to have meant much to either of the boys—they had most likely taken off for parts unknown to avoid trouble from Billy or Cherokee Bill. They'd seemed too frightened to think of stealing the cattle for themselves.

Billy rode the sorrel across belly-deep water and came out on the far bank, giving his surroundings a sweeping gaze before he started across the dry hills before him. Wind swept clouds of alkali dust into tiny swirling cyclones where no grass grew, and the dust hurt Billy's eyes.

He kept the horse in a steady trot moving away from the river, standing in his stirrups now and then to see over the next low hill. Nothing moved anywhere in sight—this part of Indian Territory was as empty as any land Billy had ever seen.

Alone with his thoughts, he passed time remembering Melissa and how she said she'd been wrong about him. He had to admit he had been wrong about her, too, although he still recalled how quick she was to get mad at him when things didn't go to suit her.

Cattle were grazing everywhere he looked, in groups of two or three, scattered all over the hills. It was easy to see that the kids had abandoned the herd to hightail it out of the country.

"I'll have to drive 'em back myself," he said, with an understanding of how difficult the chore would be. So many cows with a longhorn's temperment would be hard to drive.

He rode off to the east, making a wide circle around the cattle, pushing them together as best he could on a tired horse without any help. He'd be lucky to have the herd bunched by nightfall.

As he went about the task, he wondered about Marshal Thomas, what fate had befallen him, and there was also a chance he would run into the rustlers on his way back to the Burnet spread.

"Appears my luck has run out," he muttered, driving a white-and-black spotted cow up to the rear of the herd. The animals were more inclined to move the direction he wanted, for they could smell water, the scent coming on gusting winds from the river still many miles away. But they were still longhorns and he knew to expect the worst from them.

TWENTY-ONE

These beeves are as surly as a cowpuncher with a sticker in his boot, thought Billy, as he rode back and forth, eating dust in the dry air, trying to make the contrary animals move in the right direction.

He removed his hat and sleeved sweat off his forehead, looking up at a late-day sun, wondering just how hot and miserable he would get before he got these cattle to their home range. "Guess I've about forgotten how downright tough it is to be a cowboy, what with all that's been happenin' lately," he said to the sorrel horse. "All in all, I think I'd rather be shot at occasionally than have to try to make these hayburners do what they're supposed to."

The sorrel suddenly jumped sideways to turn a straggler, as a good cow horse was bred to do. Billy, surprised by the quick move, almost fell out of the saddle. "Damn, horse, take it easy on me . . . We got a lot of miles to cover yet," he muttered, holding onto the reins and leaning into the wind as the bronc chased the longhorn down.

The afternoon passed slowly, getting hotter and dustier as the sun set in the west. There wasn't shade worth mentioning for many miles, and Billy was caked white with the alkali dust and sand. He was relieved the cattle were getting used to being driven again after being corralled in the canyon for weeks, and they were behaving better, needing less prodding by him.

As he trailed the herd, he even had time to reflect a bit on his recent adventures. He thought back to his meeting with Marshal Thomas. Thomas had the manner of a man who could handle himself. Billy was glad he was on the right side of the law. While the marshal dressed a bit like a dandy—corduroy pants and stovepipe boots, a gaudy flannel shirt, two plated pistols with ivory handles—he had a way about him, sure moves, no wasted motion. Billy figured he'd be a hard man to take in any kind of fight, whether it was with fists or guns.

He pulled his hat down tight against a sudden gust of arid wind and spoke to himself. "Mayhaps if this ranchin' don't work out, I'll just look into becomin' a marshal. I like that kinda work—trackin' men 'stead of ornery beeves like those up ahead of me. I've been lookin' at a cow's butt for too damn many years, seems like."

The sorrel snorted against the dust and shook its head, a complaint about conditions at the rear of a herd. Billy tied his bandanna over his mouth and nose, a habit from his beginnings as a trailhand when riding drag, eating the dust from thousands of steers all the way up the Chisholm.

"This just ain't no kind of work for a grown man to be doin'," he said, his voice gentler as he thought about Melissa back at the ranch. " 'Specially if'n he ever wants to settle down somewheres with the right woman and make a home for himself."

Thinking of home and Melissa made him all the more anxious to get his journey over with, so he decided to eat in the saddle. He pulled some jerked beef and a couple of rock-hard biscuits from his saddlebags and chewed as he rode, sipping sparingly from his canteen between bites.

When he was finished eating, he pulled the sorrel to a stop and let it graze for a moment.

By the time dusk was spreading over the hills, Billy was nodding, swaying, almost asleep in his saddle. He couldn't remember when he had worked so hard for such a long stretch of time without a break. On the trail drives he had ridden, the work was difficult and strenuous, but there were always men to relieve him for short breaks to fill up on coffee or just to stretch muscles grown stiff from hours on horseback. Today, every joint in his body ached.

He trotted to the front of the herd and turned the lead animals in a tight circle, until the rest stopped walking and began to mill around, looking for tufts of sparse grass before bedding down for the night. Spooky creatures like longhorns couldn't be driven in the dark, and only an outright fool or a tinhorn would attempt it.

Billy swung down and pulled the saddle off his sorrel to make a dry camp. They were only a few miles from the river, but it was too risky to push them toward water after sundown. While he put hobbles on his horse, he again wondered about Marshal Thomas, and the whereabouts of Cherokee Bill and his sidekicks.

He looked to the south, running his tongue over dry, peeling, cracked lips. They should make the river by the middle of the morning, maybe earlier if nothing went wrong. He put his bedroll and gear on the softest piece of ground he could find, so tired he could hardly think straight.

As he lay on his ground tarp, his saddle for a pillow, Billy was relieved to see it would be a clear night. He closed his eyes a moment later and was instantly asleep, his pistol resting in his hand beside him.

He awoke, thinking he heard a noise, shivering since he'd been too tired to make a fire. He lay there, trying to remember what woke him up, clutching his blanket tight to try and keep some of the frigid night air out. The sorrel whinnied again and stomped its forefoot, as if agitated by something.

That's it, he thought, that's the sound that brought me awake—it was the gelding sensing something close by.

He raised his head slowly, trying to see what had frightened the horse. It was dark as pitch, with only faint starlight and a sliver of moon to show him his surroundings.

He realized this was no good; he simply couldn't see anything in this darkness. He eased the hammer back on his Colt and sat slowly up. He would make a fire and drive whatever critter was bothering the horse off and then he could get back to sleep, hopefully without a cattle stampede.

As he bent over to pick up some small pieces of wood and brush, he was struck from behind and bowled over to land flat on his stomach with a heavy, snarling weight on his back. He heard a growl, and all too quickly he knew what was attacking him—a big cougar that had uncharacteristically become a man-eater.

Billy knew he had only seconds to react or he was dead. He rolled to the side, bending his head forward to keep his neck out of reach. Even so, he felt his skin tear where huge fangs snapped together on his left shoulder, barely missing a deeper, fatal purchase around his throat.

Fetid breath blew in his face, and his nostrils dilated at a rancid stench of damp animal fur. Sharp pains came from his back and sides where razorlike claws dug deep, holding him as if in a lover's grasp. He dropped his pistol, knowing instinctively that if he fired, the cattle would stampede and he would never be able to round them up in this desolate country.

He jerked his skinning knife from its scabbard, reversed

the blade in his fist, and swung backhanded as hard as he could. A deep guttural grunt was followed by a whimper and the claws let go of his back as his blade drove home. Just as he turned, long teeth dug into in his left shoulder, causing him to cry out in agony, and fear.

Another quick thrust with the knife freed him. The big cat slumped over on its side, growling, struggling to get back to its feet, bleeding from two deep gashes in its belly. Legs kicking, the cougar made one last attempt to get up and then collapsed, panting, a low growl coming from its throat as its tail thrashed back and forth.

Sitting back on his haunches, breathing heavily, Billy took a closer look at the giant cat. That cougar'll go a hundred and fifty pounds easy, he thought. You were damn lucky he missed your throat on the first try; otherwise he'd be sitting here looking down at you 'stead of the other way round.

He could feel his blood running in rivulets down his left arm, the coppery smell making his stomach roll. He had come perilously close to death just now, not at the hands of outlaws, but a far more painful way to die—being eaten alive by a hungry mountain lion that had no fear of man smell.

It wasn't the first mountain lion he'd killed, but it was the first time he'd done it with a knife instead of a gun. He grabbed it by its rear paws and dragged the carcass off a little distance from the herd. "If they get a scent of you, old boy, they'll take off like scalded dogs," he said quietly, his arms still trembling from exertion. He glanced toward the herd and found some of them already on their feet after hearing the big cat growl. Then a second look at the cougar told him why the animal had risked attacking a man, its only natural enemy. An old bullet wound, festered, oozing puss, formed a swollen knot on its right front leg. A crippled cougar stood little chance of catching a rabbit or a fawn. The animal would have died from starvation in a matter of weeks.

Billy returned to his bedroll and built a small fire. He needed light to see how much damage the big cat had done to his shoulder and back. He was already starting to stiffen up and knew that if the wounds were deep, he'd have to sear them or risk infection, even death. When the fire began to crackle and hiss, he went over to his mount, calming the sorrel when it shied at the scent of cat on his clothes. He patted and stroked its neck a moment. "Easy, boy. That mountain lion was after me. It was smart enough to know a horse was too big for it to bring down."

He returned to his camp, put a small pot of water on to boil, and stripped off his shirt. The scratches on his neck and back weren't deep enough to worry about, but the two deep punctures above his left shoulder were going to be a problem. The bleeding had slowed to a mere trickle, and the holes were open enough that they should drain well, which he figured would make infection less likely. He dipped his bandanna in the steaming water and, gritting his teeth, washed out the worst of his wounds. He whistled an old trail tune through tight lips, trying not to think about the pain as he worked. Finally, after he had cleaned the injuries as well as he could, he opened his bag of Arbuckle's and poured a handful into what water was left. Hell, he thought, might as well have a little coffee since I got the water all ready.

He poured himself a cup when it smelled just about right, sat on the ground, and eased back against his saddle to build himself a cigarette. He didn't smoke often, but there were some occasions that just demanded a cigarette and this was damn sure one of them.

Closing his eyes, he took a deep drag and followed it

with a drink of coffee. It's good to be alive, he thought, even if your arm does feel like someone's put a brand on it. He leaned back and stared at the stars, breathing deeply of sagebrush-scented air, as he waited for the dawn.

TWENTY-TWO

Crossing thirsty cattle over the Red was easy, after allowing the herd to drink its fill. As Billy got them headed south, the longhorns strung out in good trail order, grazing along peacefully as they went. He counted a number of other brands on some of the cows. Cherokee Bill had raided the herds of several ranches, and here was proof he could show Marshal Thomas—if he could find the lawman again.

Billy's arm and shoulder had begun to throb, but he counted himself lucky that his horse had given him just enough warning to awaken him in time to save his skin. Good range-bred horses were like that—with keener senses than a man's and an instinct for survival that barn-raised horses never developed. Billy knew he owed the sorrel gelding his life.

Off to the southwest he could make out the flat mesa where Burnet land began, yet it was forty or fifty miles away. In this country, on a clear day, a man with good eyes could see for fifty miles, about as far as a horse could travel if its rider pushed hard.

West of the trail, a string of dry ravines wandered aim-lessly between gentle hills. Here and there were stands of oak and on occasional cedar, and far more frequent were patches of thorny mesquite clustered in low spots. Billy wondered if Heck Thomas might be lying dead or wounded in one of those dry washes, the victim of an ambush in the dark. But with a herd to take care of, there was little Billy could do to look for the marshal.

Billy made up his mind that his first responsibility went to the man who was paying him. Getting Mr. Burnet's cattle back to the ranch simply had to come ahead of looking for the marshal's tracks or his whereabouts.

Toward the middle of the afternoon, the distant pop of a handgun brought him up short. The sound had come from the west, where a cluster of dark green cedar trees stood along the edge of an arroyo. His sorrel heard it, too, pricking its ears forward, looking in the same direction. The way the wind was blowing, it could have come from a mile or more away.

"Trouble," Billy muttered. He'd be forced to let the herd scatter in order to see who was doing the shooting. Perhaps now he had an explanation for Marshal Thomas's disappearance—Thomas could be in a battle for his life surrounded by three or four outlaws.

He couldn't simply ride off without investigating the source of the gunshot. Reining his sorrel west, he kicked it to a lope and pulled his Winchester, resting the butt plate against his thigh. The wind was blowing in his face and it would help hide the sounds of his approach. If he stayed to low ground, the odds were better that whoever was doing the shooting wouldn't see him.

Keeping the cedars in sight whenever he could, he rode hard in places, slowing when he had to cross an opening where someone might notice a horse and rider. He reminded himself that he, too, could be riding into an ambush, a trap laid by Cherokee Bill for any man who tried to come to the marshal's aid.

His horse sensed something and slowed its strides on its own as they rounded a bend in a dry stream bed. Billy sawed back on the reins to bring his mount to a bounding halt. And then he saw what had spooked the sorrel. Lying on its side near a cluster of slender mesquites, a horse with a saddle cinched to its back lay in the shade of mesquite limbs. Billy needed only a second to recognize the buttermilk roan gelding belonging to Heck Thomas.

"The sumbitches shot his horse just like they done mine," he said, gritting his teeth.

He swung down, tying off his sorrel to a short cedar bush before pulling off his spurs. A quiet approach stood a far better chance of catching a gunman unawares. Ahead, the floor of the ravine was dotted with cedar bushes and mesquites. On a hunch that he'd be in some close-quarters fighting, Billy booted his Winchester and took down his Greener shotgun, pocketing a few extra loads. And to make himself harder to see, he hung his Stetson on his saddle horn. Moving forward on the balls of his feet, he crept down the bottom of the arroyo, keeping to trees and cedars wherever he could.

Around another bend in the creek bed he thought he heard the scrape of a boot. Crouching down, he inched closer to the turn, where a rocky ledge hung over the wash. Billy brought the shotgun up, resting it against his left hip as he drew his Colt revolver.

Peering cautiously around the bend, he saw a thick-shouldered man in leather chaps with a flop-brim hat less than twenty yards away, hiding behind a pile of boulders with a rifle in his hands. His skin was black. He wore a fringed buckskin shirt with beaded decorations.

Cherokee Bill, Billy thought. It *has* to be him . . .

Very slowly, placing each foot down carefully, sound-lessly, he stepped away from the rock ledge, leveling his Greener on the rifleman's back.

"Hold real still," Billy said quietly. "I've got a ten-gauge shotgun aimed at your spine. You make one move an' I'll blow you into so goddamn many pieces somebody'll need a garden rake to gather you up."

The big man tensed. He turned his head slowly to see who was behind him. He had a broad, flat face and close-set dark eyes narrowed with hatred. His gaze dropped to the twin barrels of Billy's Greener.

"That's right," Billy said, thumbing back both hammers on his shotgun. "Mighty big holes for gun barrels, ain't they? I can't miss from here. You'll be Cherokee Bill, an' unless you put that Winchester down real slow, you're gonna be the late Cherokee Bill. What's left of him."

He was reading Billy's face now, looking for signs of doubt or worry. "An' jus' who might you be?" his thick voice asked.

"Name's Billy Blue. I killed two of your boys—French an' McWilliams. Dropped a couple more night before last at the Burnet Ranch. Never bothered askin' their names. An' I'm gonna kill you, Cherokee Bill, unless you drop that rifle right now."

Bill hesitated. "That marshal over yonder's gonna hang me if'n I give myself up, so's I'm a dead man either way."

"Most likely," Billy replied. "One thing you can be real sure of—you're one dead son of a bitch right now if you don't drop that gun. Truth is, I'd enjoy killin' you myself, because of the pair of Burnet cowboys you an' your boys shot down, two good men whose only job was tendin' to cows. You gunned 'em down an' they didn't stand a chance. Just thinkin' about it now makes me want to pull both these goddamn triggers."

"You're bluffin'."

Billy wagged his head. "Never bluffed a man in my life."

"What stake you got in this, Blue?"

"A payday. I work for Mr. Burke Burnet. Now, stop talkin' an' drop that rifle, or I'm gonna show you what it's like to turn into a bunch of little bitty pieces."

"I'll make you a deal," Bill said, staring into Billy's eyes. "I got a hundred head of cattle across that river. I'll give you half if'n you let me go."

"You ain't got 'em anymore, you murderin' bastard. I took 'em back from them two kids, Tommy an' Charlie. I drove 'em all this way. They're maybe a mile east of us right now, so you ain't got no more tradin' stock. No deal. This is the last time I'm gonna say it—drop the gun or you can kiss your ass goodbye."

"Shit," Bill whispered, as he let his Winchester slide from his hands. He still carried a pistol belted around his waist.

"Now, take out the Colt with your thumb an' forefinger. If it don't come out of that holster just right, there's gonna be a red puddle an' a bunch of bones where you're standin' now."

"You ain't got a chance, white boy," Bill growled. "I got a bunch of my men all round you."

"Two or three," Bill answered. "Won't matter to you 'cause you'll be dead if just one of 'em shows his face. Soon as you put that pistol on the ground, you're gonna tell 'em to give themselves up."

"An if I don't?" Bill asked, eyelids slitting even more.

"Then I'll blow you in half an' tell Marshal Thomas you was tryin' to get away. He'll believe me. We're acquainted, me an' the marshal, you see. He told me the law had been tryin' to catch you for years. I'll be doin' everybody a favor. Might get a big reward, too. Hell, I've damn near gone an' talked myself into killin' you anyhow."

For the first time, there was fear in Cherokee Bill's eyes, and he reached slowly for the butt of his pistol with his thumb and forefinger. "You're a crazy man," he said, taking out his gun and letting it fall with a thud beside his right boot.

"Maybe," Billy said, half a smile lifting one corner of his mouth. "Or maybe I just enjoy killin' folks who need killin'. Now, turn around an' start yellin' to your boys to lay down their weapons. Tell 'em if they don't come out with empty hands raised real high where I can see 'em, I'm gonna turn you into chunks of fishbait before me an' the marshal start comin' after them."

"Sweet Jesus," Bill said softly, making a quarter turn to face down the draw. "You gotta be the craziest white boy I ever run across."

Heck Thomas had a deep thigh wound. He was scarcely able to stand while Billy lined up Cherokee Bill and two more rustlers in a basin where the arroyo widened. Billy held his shotgun on all three men while Thomas tied Billy's bandanna around his upper leg to stem the blood flow.

"They killed my horse," Thomas said, grimacing when he tied the knot securely. "It was dark as hell when they ambushed me an' I didn't see a thing till it was too late. I've been standin' 'em off all day, runnin' low on water an' ammunition. Sure glad you came along when you did."

"I heard a gunshot while I was drivin' Mr. Burnet's stolen cattle back to the ranch. Rode over to investigate. I guess I got lucky, slippin' up on Cherokee Bill's back the way I did."

Thomas nodded and picked up his rifle, limping over to the spot where Billy held the rustlers at gunpoint. He gave Cherokee Bill a cold stare. "We've been after this sumbitch for a long time. I've got four sets of wrist irons in my saddlebags behind that dead horse. I'd be obliged if you'd fetch three sets for me. We're gonna put bracelets on these boys an' then find where they hid their horses. We'll take 'em the rest of the way to Burke's ranch, only Cherokee Bill, otherwise known as Mr. Crawford Goldsby, is gonna walk every damn step of the way. He's the son of a bitch who shot my roan."

"Sounds like a good idea to me," Billy said, remembering the good chestnut gelding Cherokee Bill shot out from under him at the ranch that night. "Might be even better if ol' Bill took his walk without any boots. Since he's gonna hang, don't reckon it matters if he's a little sore-footed when he climbs up them gallows steps."

Marshal Thomas grinned. "I like the way your brain works, Mr. Blue. Soon as you get back with them manacles, we'll have Goldsby pull off his boots . . . see how well he travels in his bare feet across some of this cactus."

Cherokee Bill glared at the marshal, but when he looked at Billy he quickly looked the other way.

"Be right back with those cuffs," Billy said.

Marshal Thomas raised his rifle, aiming it at the three outlaws. "No hurry," he said. "These boys ain't goin' no place now . . . not without some holes in 'em, they ain't."

Billy strode back down the arroyo, balancing his shotgun in his palm. A thought occurred to him as he went for the wrist irons—Cherokee Bill hadn't turned out to be all that tough after all, despite his bad reputation. Like Leon Pickett, he'd failed to live up to what folks said about him, when the chips were down.

TWENTY-THREE

Marshal Thomas sat aboard a tall black gelding with a U.S. Army brand on its flank, an animal stolen from some cavalry post or a picket line while the army was on patrol. Thomas was in a great deal of pain sitting a saddle with a thigh wound, but he did his best not to show it.

Billy led two brown geldings, tied head and tail, behind him with each horse carrying a sullen-faced member of Cherokee Bill's gang, his hands cuffed behind him. Both were Indians, judging by their facial features. Cherokee Bill Goldsby walked in front of Marshal Thomas in his stocking feet, mincing over sharp rocks, avoiding cactus patches, his arms also bound behind him by wrist irons.

''Makes a real pretty sight, don't it?'' the marshal asked, inclining his head toward the outlaw leader, keeping his rifle on the rustler's back as they moved slowly along the bottom of a ravine. ''Ol' Goldsby can be real light-footed when he has to be. I'm enjoyin' the hell outta this.''

Billy grinned, his shotgun resting across the pommel of his saddle. ''Ever since I got to this part of the country, folks have been tellin' me how tough Cherokee Bill was, how he was such a bad hombre. Don't appear anybody knew the bottoms of his feet was so tender. I reckon you could say he's got a soft spot or two . . . They just ain't in the right places.''

At that, Thomas chuckled. ''You've got a cowboy's sense of humor, Billy. I did my share of punchin' cows when I was a bit younger. A man's gotta learn to laugh at damn near everything that goes wrong around a herd of cows, which can be damn near everything. Only we ain't herdin' cows just now. Thanks to you, we've got a herd of cow thieves. Besides that, you've earned yourself a five-hundred-dollar reward for the capture of Crawford Goldsby. It won't make you a rich man, but I'd imagine you can find a way to spend it. I'll have to send a wire to Fort Smith to get authorization for a bank to pay you. It's liable to take a few weeks.''

''Five hundred dollars?'' Billy exclaimed. It sounded like all the money in the world.

''For a fact. You caught the bastard, so it's your money.''

Billy shook his head. ''Don't hardly know what to say. I've never had five hundred dollars to spend. Seems like I must be dreamin'.''

''You ain't dreamin', son. This barefooted bastard is one real dangerous son of a bitch. Plenty of bounty hunters have tried to catch him, or kill him. That reward was good alive or dead. Judge Parker is gonna enjoy hangin' him. I'll have to admit I'm gonna be mighty happy to watch him swing from the end of a rope. My partner, Marshal Bill Tilghman, will be glad to hear the news himself. We've tracked this slippery bastard all over the Nations for a couple of years.''

Hearing this, Cherokee Bill glanced over his shoulder to give Billy a steely-eyed look. He had opened his mouth to say something when one of his feet struck a rock. ''Eee-yow!'' he cried, hopping on the other foot a few times before he resumed his careful footsteps down the draw without looking back or saying a word.

"He can damn near sing, too," Billy observed dryly. "If he wasn't headed for a gallows, I'd recommend him for a place in a church choir."

Some of the marshal's good humor left him when he said, "I imagine he's gonna make some chokin' sounds before too long," a hard expression crossing his face. "There'll be plenty of cowmen who'll be grateful to hear about it."

Billy led his prisoners up a slight incline out of the draw, to a flat plain where the stolen cattle grazed, scattered as far as the eye could see. "I'll have to come back with Juan to help me get these cows to the ranch. Some has got different brands an' we'll need some help findin' their legal owners."

"I can help with that," Thomas offered. "We can track most recorded brands through the cattlemen's association. Maybe Burke will recognize some of 'em."

"I hadn't thought of that," Billy said. "Some of these cows could belong to his neighbors."

"How'd you get all those cuts on your arm an' shoulder?" the marshal asked. "Looks like you lost an argument with a bad-tempered woman."

"A crippled mountain lion tried to have me for supper last night. It had an old wound on one leg. Big cat, too, maybe a hundred an' fifty pounds. I reckon it was so hungry it didn't pay no attention to my smell."

"Downright unusual," Thomas agreed. "Most cougars stay wide of a man, when they can."

"It sure as hell took me by surprise. I've hunted a few big cats that developed at taste for baby calves, but I ain't never had one come huntin' me."

Thomas waited until Cherokee Bill had climbed out of the ravine before he spoke again. "You've proved to be real capable handlin' law-breakin' men. If you'd be interested in a deputy marshal's job, I'd sure as hell recommend you to my boss, Marshal Evett Nix."

"Hadn't really thought about it much," Billy told him. "I appreciate the offer anyhow."

"Think it over, son. The pay ain't all that good and a man sure spends a lot of time in a saddle. But it has its good side. Like when you end the careers of rustlers an' killers like this bunch. Makes a man feel good about what he's doin'."

Billy's thoughts drifted to Melissa. "To tell the truth I'm kinda tired of movin' around. If I could find the right piece of ground to raise some cattle of my own, an' maybe a good woman to start a family with, I might be ready to settle down. That five-hundred-dollar reward would help me get started."

"There's forks in every man's road, Billy. You choose the one you think'll take you where you'd like to be." He scowled at Cherokee Bill. "An' then some pick what looks like the easiest way to get what they want, but if it means breakin' the law, they usually wind up dead, or behind bars, like these boys are gonna be. I'll see to it you're invited to the hangin' when Judge Parker stretches Mr. Goldsby's neck."

A hanging was something Billy didn't care to see, although he said nothing about it to Marshal Thomas as they aimed southwest, toward the ranch.

TWENTY-FOUR

He sat beside Melissa on a bench on the front porch after supper. A cool spring night offered up gentle breezes. A week had passed since Heck Thomas rode off with four prisoners, including one badly wounded outlaw and Cherokee Bill Goldsby, in the company of a six-man squad of soldiers Juan summoned from Fort Sill by wire. The marshal's leg still pained him, after eight days of recovery under Mrs. Burnet's care while he waited for the soldiers.

Juan and Pia were down at the barns watching a mare give birth to a foal. Ever since Billy got back to the ranch, Melissa had shown him an extra amount of attention, a fact that had not escaped Mrs. Burnet's notice, though she seemed to approve, smiling when Billy was offered an extra slice of pie or plum cobbler by her daughter after the supper dishes were cleared away. But when Billy was alone with Melissa, it seemed the words he wanted to say got stuck in his mouth somehow. As they had tonight, sitting on the porch with her, both of them silent for long periods of time.

"Dad should be back in a couple of weeks," Melissa said, after a silence that seemed to last much too long. "I know he'll be proud of what you did to get our cattle back. He won't be happy to hear about Luis and Lincoln. They had been with us for quite a while . . . Luis a few years longer than Lincoln, the best I remember.''

''Seems like there's always some bad news to go along with the good,'' he said. ''Most times, anyway.'' Billy wondered why talking to Melissa seemed so difficult now. He *wanted* to say all the right things to her, but when the time came to get them said he developed a bad case of lockjaw.

''Will you be staying on here with us?'' she asked in a timid voice, hard to hear despite the night quiet blanketing the ranch.

''I reckon that'll be up to Mr. Burnet,'' he answered. ''To tell the honest truth, I'd sure like to stay.''

''I hope you will, Billy.''

He glanced over at her, thankful that the darkness would hide a flush creeping into his face. ''If it don't seem improper to say so, Melissa, the main reason I'd like to stay here is on account of you.''

''That isn't improper at all,'' she whispered, and then she reached across the bench for his hand. ''I'm flattered.''

Billy cleared his throat. The touch of her hand sent a tingle down his spine. He wasn't bashful around other women, for the most part, and he pondered why he was having such a hard time being at ease with her. ''I'm not all that good when it comes to talking to girls,'' he began, forcing each word across his tongue, ''but there's a couple of things I'd like to say. First is, you're about the prettiest girl I ever laid eyes on. I know I'm just an ordinary cowboy an' you're the daughter of a rich rancher, so you most likely wouldn't have no interest in havin' me keep company with you in a regular way. But if me bein' a cowhand don't bother you all that much, I'd like to take you for a ride sometime. Maybe go to Wichita Falls in the buckboard to buy you a pretty dress, soon as that reward money comes."

"Why, Billy. That's so sweet of you. But I don't need a new dress. What I'd really like is to take that ride you were talking about . . . maybe some evening when the moon is full."

"Sure sounds good to me. You're right sure it don't make any difference that I'm not a rich man?"

"Not a bit of difference. Money isn't everything. Not to me."

"What'll Miz Burnet an' your pa say?"

She smiled. "Ma already knows I like you . . . in a special sort of way. She teases me about it, how I look at you differently sometimes."

"I hadn't noticed," he lied. She *had* been staring at him more often lately.

Melissa giggled. "Ma says you've been looking at me when my back is turned sometimes. She pays attention to that sort of thing. I wasn't going to tell you. Ma said you'd be embarrassed if I did."

"Maybe a little," he admitted, "but Mr. Burnet is liable to think I'm steppin' out of line."

Melissa's smile widened. "You leave Pa to me. Ma says I've always been Daddy's girl, that I've got him wrapped around my little finger. I'll talk to him when he gets back. He'll understand."

"I ain't so sure," Billy said, remembering the stone-faced rancher who hired him.

Without being asked, Melissa scooted a little closer to him on the bench, still holding his palm, squeezing it gently as she stared into his face. She seemed to be waiting for something.

Taking a big chance, Billy leaned over and kissed her on the lips very lightly, wondering if he might be pushing his luck by trying a kiss so soon.

To his surprise, she kissed him back, leaving her mouth

over his even longer than he would have hoped.

"That was nice," he said, when she drew her lips away. "I might get to where I was real fond of your kisses."

"I already like giving them to you, Billy. I've told you this before. When we first met, I thought you were sort of cocky, like you had a high opinion of yourself. After I got to know you, I found out I was wrong. You can be a gentle man, although I've seen what you can do when you're angry . . . when you're mad enough to use your gun."

"I was only doin' my job, Melissa . . . what Mr. Burnet hired me to do."

"I understand. Maybe . . . It's hard to put into words, but I think you can be two different people. I know you've killed men with your guns, but when you are around me and my ma, you're as gentle as a lamb."

He grinned. "Never was called a lamb before."

"You know what I mean. You have a gentle side."

"I reckon. Never thought about it all that much. Not till just lately."

"Have you been thinking about me lately."

He was sure his face was the color of blood when she asked the question. "No sense denyin' it. I've thought about you a lot."

"And what have you been thinking?"

Something fluttered inside his chest and his heart was beating faster now. "How I'd like to take that reward money an' buy a little spread of my own. Maybe a few cows to start with. Build a little house . . . It wouldn't be much to begin with 'cause I won't have hardly enough money." He found he couldn't look at her just then.

"And then what would you do?" she asked.

From the corner of his eye he could see her smiling. "I'd work up the nerve . . . might take some time . . . an' then I'd ask you to marry me. I figure you'll say no the first couple of hundred times; only I'd keep on askin' till you said yes.''

She put her fingertips over her mouth to suppress a giggle. ''What makes you so sure I'd say no?''

Billy looked down at his badly worn boots. '' 'Cause you're a rich man's daughter an' I'm just a cowboy. If I bought a little parcel of land an' built the house myself, an' paid for a few cows, I'd be flat busted again, just like I am now. A rich man's daughter wouldn't like bein' broke.''

''You sound like you think you're an authority on rich men's daughters. Have you ever known one?''

''Nope. Never met one, really, till I met you.''

''Then how can you be so sure how I'd feel about starting out without any money?''

He stared off at the dark prairie a moment. ''You're used to havin' nice things . . . good clothes to wear, plenty to eat, that sort of thing. I couldn't guarantee you that. If there came a dry year, a few cows wouldn't make any money. We'd have to live out of what we could raise in a garden. Might even go hungry, an' I know you ain't used to it.''

''You sound so sure I'd be unhappy if times got hard.''

''Just guessin', I suppose. This is real hard for me to talk about. It's like admittin' I might not be able to keep you happy if my plans didn't work out.''

Now Melissa gave the hills around the ranch a lingering look while she chewed thoughtfully on her bottom lip. ''We didn't have money to start with,'' she said. ''When I was a little girl, my pa had to fight off Comanches and worry about dry years and all the same things you said you'd worry about. Dad made this ranch into something we're all proud of, and he didn't start with a lot of money.''

He felt her squeeze his hand again. ''I just wouldn't want to disappoint you,'' he said.

She looked at him. ''Do you know what love is, Billy? Do you know what it means?''

''I think I do. It means you care for somebody with all your heart no matter what.''

''Exactly. Being poor has nothing to do with love.''

He met her level gaze, hoping what he'd already said didn't sound too foolish. He was about to say a great deal more. ''I know I could love you for the rest of my life, Melissa Burnet, if you didn't mind bein' poor to start with.''

She leaned toward him and kissed his cheek, a mere peck, and then she spoke in a whisper. ''I love you, William Jackson Blue. Rich or poor. I know we'd be happy together.''

Billy let go of her hand and put his arms around her. ''I'm real sure I'd be the happiest cowboy in Texas if you'd decide to be my wife.''

''I've already decided. I'll marry you whenever you're ready to ask.''

''I'll have to speak to Mr. Burnet first, to get his permission in order to do it proper.''

''I know he'll give his permission,'' she said.

''He hardly even knows me. He saw me shoot down a gunfighter, an' on account of that, he offered me this job. He might not want his daughter marryin' a man who has blood on his hands.''

''I'll talk to him, and so will Ma. She likes you, and she knows what you did to help us while Dad was away. I heard her talking to Marshal Thomas. The marshal said you were a brave man and that you could be trusted. Dad knows Marshal Thomas. What the marshal said will carry a lot of weight with my pa.''

''You'd make me a mighty happy man if you'd agree to marry me, Melissa.''

''I've already agreed. Let's go for a walk. We've done enough talking for now . . .''

AUTHOR'S NOTE

The period of the late 1880s was a turbulent, lawless time in the Western United States. Though Billy Blue is a fictional character, he is an amalgam of the thousands of young men whose experiences in the Civil War made them restless and unwilling to settle for life back on the farm. These boys—white, black, and Mexican—headed for the frontier, hoping for a more exciting and fulfilling life. Most ended up being cowboys, but many made their living with a gun.

Burke Burnet was a real rancher who owned thousands of acres in North Texas and his ranch carried the 6666 brand. Legend has it the brand was so named because Burnet won the land in a poker game with four sixes, but he neither confirmed nor denied the tale. It is certain he was plagued by rustlers, as was every cattleman of the period, but history doesn't record whether Cherokee Bill ever raided the 6666 spread.

United States Marshals Heck Thomas and Bill Tilghman were authentic Western heros. Between 1892 and 1894, a young protégé of the Dalton brothers, Bill Doolin, formed a gang of ten seasoned holdup men and planned and executed a series of raids on banks and trains in Arkansas, Kansas, Missouri, and Indian Territory. Because of the outlaws' base in Indian Territory, the efforts of lawmen were coordinated by the U.S. Marshal for the territory, Evett Nix. Working in concert with Hanging Judge Isaac Parker, Nix had a flair for recruiting talent. The first aide he enlisted was Deputy U.S. Marshal Heck Thomas. A native Georgian, Thomas was only twelve years old when he served as a Confederate Army courier. After the war, while working as a private detective in Texas, he pulled off the single-handed capture of two desperados, and gained a reputation among lawbreakers as a man to be avoided. When Heck Thomas came to Judge Parker's jurisdiction, he quickly impressed onlookers with his distinctive garb—knee-high boots, corduroy trousers, and flannel shirt, set off with two ivory-handled six-shooters and a well-used shotgun.

After hiring Heck Thomas, Marshal Nix recruited two more hard men for the campaign against Bill Doolin and his gang. The first was a red-haired soldier of fortune named Chris Madsen, the second was Bill Tilghman. Tilghman had chalked up a distinguished gunfighting record as marshal of Dodge City before moving to Indian Territory. The badge he wore in Dodge was a work of art hammered out of two $20 gold pieces, an insignia famous throughout the frontier. Such showmanship was characteristic of Tilghman.

Bill Tilghman, Heck Thomas, and Chris Madsen were soon dubbed the "Oklahoma Guardsmen," and were each assigned a different slice of Doolin's various stomping grounds, coordinated by Marshal Nix. Tilghman's capture of Doolin, his escape, and subsequent killing by Heck Thomas with his shotgun makes for fascinating reading and deserves its own story.

Crawford "Cherokee Bill" Goldsby was born at Fort

Concho, Texas, in 1876. His father was a black soldier and his mother was a half-black and half-Cherokee woman. When he was two years old, his father deserted the army and hid out in Indian Territory, leaving his son in the care of an elderly "aunt," Amanda Foster. After being moved about for some years, Crawford returned to live with his mother and stepfather at Fort Gibson at the age of twelve. Crawford and his stepfather did not get along, and the young man began to hang out with unsavory characters, drink liquor, and rebel against authority.

Crawford's first serious trouble started when he was eighteen. One night while attending a dance in the Fort Gibson area, he and Jake Lewis, a thirty-five-year-old black man, had a confrontation. In the fistfight, Lewis severely beat Crawford. Two days later, Crawford faced Lewis with a sixshooter and shot the unarmed man twice. Crawford fled to the Creek and Seminole Nations and joined up with two noted outlaws, Jim and Bill Cook, described as mixed-blood Cherokees.

On the evening of July 18, 1894, a gunfight occurred between Sheriff Ellis Gourd and a posse of seven men on one side and the Cooks and Goldsby on the other. Two of the posse were killed, and the rest fled. After this incident, Goldsby began to go by the name Cherokee Bill.

For several months in 1884, the Cook gang and Cherokee Bill spread terror throughout Indian Territory and Missouri and the Cherokee and Creek Nations. The gang now consisted of Jim and Bill Cook, Cherokee Bill Goldsby, Jim French, Sam McWilliams (known as the Verdigris Kid), Texas Jack, and a gunman known only as Skeeter.

Cherokee Bill was credited with most of the murders that occurred during the gang's rampage. Many times he killed for no apparent cause or reason. The number of his victims ranges from seven to fourteen, depending upon the source.

Cherokee Bill continued to be elusive, and many lawmen

were reluctant to confront him face-to-face because of his feared reputation as being one of the toughest desperados in the area. It was said he could shoot faster than two ordinary men. Using his rifle, he could hit a squirrel in the eye as far as he could see and could shoot from his waist and hardly ever miss his target. The citizens of one town he frequented, Lenapah, were so afraid of him, an ordinance was passed granting him the privilege of free movement without being molested, one of the most unusual acts in the history of the Western frontier.

Finally, with the help of one of his "friends," U.S. marshals arrested Cherokee Bill in April of 1895. Taken before Judge Isaac Charles "Hanging Judge" Parker, he was charged with murder and convicted and sentenced to hang. When his mother and sister, who had been in the courtroom throughout the trial, wept loudly, Cherokee Bill smiled and said, "What's the matter with you two? I ain't dead yet."

Somehow, a .45-caliber revolver and nine cartridges were smuggled into Cherokee Bill's cell, some say by Henry Starr, grandson of Cherokee outlaw Tom Starr and nephew of Sam Starr.

On July 26, 1895, at 7:00 in the evening, Turnkey Campbell Eoff and Guard Lawrence Keating entered Murderer's Row. While passing Cherokee Bill's cell, Keating was shot and killed after he disobeyed Bill's order to give up his weapon. Eoff ran up the corridor and Bill stepped from his cell and fired twice. George Pearce, another outlaw and one of the plot's ringleaders, ran after Eoff. This probably saved Eoff's life, because Cherokee Bill could not shoot him without hitting Pearce.

Cherokee Bill held the jail under siege and began firing at random from his cell. Each time he would fire, he would gobble, a sound somewhere between the bark of a coyote and the call of a turkey. The prisoners were badly frightened and many had crawled under their bunks or huddled in the corner of their cells. Cherokee Bill continued to hold out and refused to surrender.

Henry Starr volunteered to go into Bill's cell and attempt to talk him into giving up the weapon. A short time later, Starr emerged from the cell with Bill's pistol.

A second trial was held and Cherokee Bill was again sentenced to hang by Judge Parker on March 17, 1896.

Shortly after 2 P.M. while on the gallows, it was reported Cherokee Bill was asked if he had anything to say. He replied, "I came here to die, not make a speech." Approximately twelve minutes later Crawford "Cherokee Bill" Goldsby, the most notorious outlaw in the Territory, was dead.